KT-441-353

WHERE LOVE BELONGS

Lizzie Vale, Nellie Cobridge's youngest sibling, has to make a decision. What will she do with her life? Journalism excites her, but in 1938 it's not easy for a woman to get a job in this field, however bright and lively she is. Determined to succeed, she tries various schemes and tackles everything with enthusiasm. Fortunately, she has the support of a loving family when things go wrong. She meets Charlie and her future seems set. Or is it?

CHRISSIE LOVEDAY

WHERE LOVE BELONGS

Complete and Unabridged

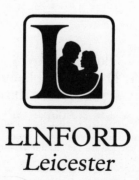

LINFORD
Leicester

First published in Great Britain in 2011

First Linford Edition
published 2012

British Library CIP Data

Loveday, Chrissie.
Where love belongs. - -
(Linford romance library)
1. Love stories.
2. Large type books.
I. Title II. Series
823.9'2–dc23

ISBN 978–1–4448–1290–9

Published by
F. A. Thorpe (Publishing)
Anstey, Leicestershire

Set by Words & Graphics Ltd.
Anstey, Leicestershire
Printed and bound in Great Britain by
T. J. International Ltd., Padstow, Cornwall

This book is printed on acid-free paper

The Potteries, 1938

Nellie opened the note, recognising her mother's untidy scrawl and wondering why on earth she had written at all.

I think you'd better come right away. It's your dad. Been took bad, he has. Love, your mother.

'Thank you, Davy. Here's tuppence for your trouble.' She handed the coins over to the little boy, son of her mother's neighbour.

Her father must be really ill if her mother found it necessary to send a note and didn't come round in person. She called out, 'I have to go out, Mrs Potts. My father's ill, apparently.'

The housekeeper looked worried.

'I'm sorry to hear that, Mrs Cobridge. Hope he's soon better. Your mother said he wasn't too good when I spoke to her last time she came round.'

'Really? She didn't tell me.'

'Yes, well, she didn't want to worry you, I suppose. She came through and had a cup of tea with me one afternoon.'

'I see. Well now, Mr James is supposed to be coming home for his lunch. I don't know how long I'll be away, but you can ask Cook to keep something back for me. Oh dear, it would happen today. I've got so many things I wanted to do. That's life, I suppose.'

Nellie put her coat and hat on and went out to her little car. The Standard Eight was her pride and joy. She had taken to driving like a duck to water and felt as if she'd grown a new pair of arms and legs with the time it saved her.

No more having to walk to places and waiting for buses. She drove the short distance to her mother's house and parked in the road outside. There was the familiar twitch of the net curtain from the house next door.

'Oh Nellie, thank you for coming.

2

I'm that worried. I can't get your dad to say anything. I reckon he's had one of them there strokes.'

Nan Vale looked every one and more of her sixty-four years. Though her life had been easier since Nellie had married James Cobridge, heir to one of the major pot banks in Longton; the early years of hardship had taken their toll on her mother.

'Let's have a look at him, then,' Nellie said sharply. 'The sooner we can get medical attention, the better it will be. I nearly phoned James's uncle before I left, but thought I'd better take a look at him first. Are you in by yourself?'

'Yes, love. Lizzie's gone off out somewhere. Now she's finished her schooling, she's always off out somewhere.'

The two women went upstairs. Nellie was horrified at the look of her father. His breathing was laboured and he lay with his eyes closed. They obviously needed a doctor and luckily, there was one in the family.

'Oh, Mum. I'm afraid there isn't much we can do for him. I'll go home and phone James's Uncle Henry and get back as soon as I can. I just hope he won't be out on his rounds. I wish you'd let us install a telephone for you. It would save so much time.'

'I wouldn't mind that much, but your dad was always dead against it. Says we've had enough charity from your husband.'

'Nonsense. You've always paid your way. Look Mum, I think you need to prepare yourself. I think you're right and he's had a stroke. He does look in a bad way. Will you be all right while I go and get the doctor?'

'I reckon so. Your dad's going, isn't he?'

'I think so, Mum. I'll leave you for a bit, but I'll be back as soon as I can.'

'Funny to think of him lying there so feeble, after being such big man all his life.'

'I know. I'll be back soon.'

With mixed emotions, she drove back to her home and made the call to the doctor. Her father had been a difficult man. Granted he'd mellowed a bit in his last years, but he still ruled his wife and the children living at home with a rod of iron.

She still remembered the difficult days of her own teenage years when she was almost single-handedly supporting her brothers and sister as well as sick parents. Seeing him lying there, a defeated, crumpled old man seemed all wrong. It wasn't her father any more.

★　★　★

Two days later, his life ended. The funeral was held with due ceremony, a week later. The mourners, such as there were, went back to Nellie and James's house for the wake.

Apart from the family, a couple of old friends from the Miners' Social club had attended along with two of their neighbours. These four had left when the ham sandwiches and currant loaf were finished.

In keeping with Nan's strict beliefs, there was no alcohol served. She had signed the pledge many years before and had fought long and hard to keep her sons away from the demon drink. They rarely did drink alcohol in her presence as a mark of respect, but they certainly did not keep this up when they were away from her.

'So, the start of a new era,' James said to the family. 'You all have my sympathy and I know you will miss him in your own ways. I trust you will be happy to stay in your house, Nan. It's yours rent free for as long as you want to live there. If you prefer to move somewhere smaller, I'm sure we can arrange it. Our company still has a number of properties around the area.

'Or you may like to move in here with us. I think Nellie would be pleased to have you, if you should accept.'

Nellie nodded, though she did have some reservations about the idea.

'Oh that's very good of you, James, but I couldn't do that,' Nan replied. 'I couldn't live with anyone doing things for me all the time. It's all right for our Nellie, having maids and cooks and everything, but I couldn't be doing with it. Not at all. Besides, where would our Ben and Lizzie live?' The young man looked up.

'Actually Mum, I was thinking of moving out myself. A couple of the lads I work with, well, we were all thinking that we might try to get a place of our own. You know, sharing costs and all.'

'And I could be going off somewhere soon, as well,' Lizzie chimed in.

'My goodness. It really is the end of everything, isn't it?' Nan wailed. 'I might as well follow Enoch into the grave. I'm no use any more. Not wanted by any of you. Nellie away and married with a kiddy of her own. Joe and Daisy off in their own cottage and practically running the Baines's farm. I've got nowt left, have I? Not if you young ones are planning to go an all.'

There was silence around the table for a moment. Nobody could think of anything to say.

'Of course you must come and live here with us, Mum. You'll be able to help me looking after William and run the house. I'm going to be working longer hours soon.'

'But William will be going away to school in October,' James interrupted. 'Oh, of course you can come here, Nan. I said so, didn't I? But not to look after William. I've arranged for him to go away to board at my old prep school.'

'We'll talk about this later, James,' Nellie hissed. It was an old bone of contention. She certainly did not want her precious son sent away to boarding school.

Her husband was glaring at her but wisely, he did not pursue the argument in front of her family. The boy was only eight years old and still her baby. Their wish for another child had never materialised. Nobody could explain it or offer a solution, so it seemed he was destined to be an only one.

'So what are your plans, Lizzie?' James asked. 'Have you thought what you want to do with your life? You've got some good qualifications. You could go to college or university perhaps. Become a teacher?'

'I don't know. Don't think I'd be any good as a teacher.'

Lizzie had recently passed her Higher School Certificate, the first in her family ever to achieve anything academically. James had been trying to encourage her to continue her education, but she and her brothers all thought it was time she was earning a wage. Besides, she was feeling restless and wanted to see something of life outside her home town, not get tied to going to the local university or training college.

'Haven't you got any idea of what you want to do?' Nellie asked a touch sharply.

'Not really. I'm quite good at English. I liked doing composition.

Maybe I could work on the newspapers or something.'

'Maybe I could have a word with the editor of the Evening Post. I meet him regularly at one of my clubs.'

'Is there anyone you don't know?' Ben said. 'Strikes me, once you're a boss of something, you always know someone.'

Ben worked at the Cobridge factory. Though he was keen on design, like his sister, Nellie, he had chosen to specialise in the clay end and had become an expert thrower. His hands could magic the solid lumps of clay into beautifully shaped vases and jugs, achieving some of the best results of anyone in the factory.

'You might be right. Once you're in something like the Rotary Club, you tend to meet other people on the same level. Keeps you in touch with all the businesses in the area. Not that it's always a good thing to know what's going on. Can be very depressing at times.'

10

'Right, well I think we'd better get back to the farm,' Joe announced. Me and Daisy have got to get the herd in ready for milking. Her dad doesn't do the milking any more so it's down to us.'

'Thanks for the tea and everything,' Daisy said shyly. She was still somewhat in awe of her sister-in-law and husband, with their large house and a number of servants.

She couldn't wait to get back to their little cottage on her father's farm, a place where she felt completely comfortable and in charge. One day soon, she hoped they might have a family of their own and her happiness would be complete. They had decided to wait much longer than she might have wished before starting a family, but now the time was ripe.

Her beloved Joe, their life on the farm and children playing around in the garden. What could be better? 'You can always come and stay with us, Lizzie, if you wanted a break in the country for a bit. I'm sure we could find plenty for you to do on the farm.'

'Thanks Daisy, but I think life among the cows would terrify me. They're such great big things, lumbering around the place.'

'We don't exactly have them inside the cottage, little sister,' Joe laughed. 'You'd be quite safe. They're really quite gentle creatures. Just the bull you have to be wary of. He can be a bit bad tempered sometimes.' He made a roaring sound and they all smiled.

'Yes, well thanks a lot, but I think I'll give it some more thought before I commit to being a farm hand.'

'Well, the offer's there if you just wanted a little holiday in the country. And Mum, you could always come and stay with us for a bit of you'd like to. Come on now Daisy, love, we'd best be getting back or your dad'll never lend us his precious car ever again.'

'It's been lovely to see you, even if it is because of a sad occasion. Come again soon,' Nellie said as she kissed her brother and sister-in-law. She waved them off and returned to the diminishing funeral party in the drawing room. 'Now, will I tell Cook you'll stay for some dinner?'

'Yes please,' said Ben.

'We'd best be getting back,' Nan said at exactly the same time.

'What's to get back for? And they do a good spread here, don't you agree, our Lizzie?' Ben was already relishing the thought of dining with the company's owner, even if it was his own brother-in-law. He was never given any privileges at the factory because he was a relative, but he was happy enough with that. But now his main concern was that he felt hungry and also he knew there wasn't much to eat back at home. His mother had been pretty well out of it since his dad had passed on and decent meals had gone by the board.

'I'll go and tell Cook you'll be staying. We can eat a bit earlier than usual so you won't be too late going home,' Nellie decided.

'Won't it be short notice for her with these extra mouths to feed?'

'Course not, Mum. I told her to do a roast in case anyone stayed on. It's just a case of some extra vegetables and I know there's a big apple pie for afters.'

James went off to his study and Nan and Nellie sat down for a chat. There was a lot to be decided.

'Is it all right if me and Ben go for a walk round the garden?' Lizzie asked.

'Course you can, love. You can collect William and take him with you if you like. He's been back from school for a bit now and Jenny's been looking after him.'

Jenny was the nursemaid who had come to look after their son when he was just a tiny baby, but still looked after him when needed.

She had stayed on to help out as a general maid and served at the table when they had a large dinner party. She was only a year or so older than Lizzie, so they had become friends of a sort.

'Hello, Lizzie. Ben. I was sorry to hear about your dad. William, come here, love. Your auntie and uncle are here to see you.'

'Hiya, William. You coming out into the garden with us?'

'Yes please, Ben. I mean, Uncle Ben.'

'Just Ben's good enough for me. Have you got a football somewhere? We can have a kick about if you like.'

'Yes, please. Can I, Jenny?'

'Course you can, dear. I'll just get my coat and I'll take a walk round with you. If you don't mind?'

Lizzie grinned. She suspected Jenny had more than a soft spot for her brother. It was about time he was walking out with someone and Jenny was a lovely girl. So kind hearted and very good with William.

It was all a bit strange. Funny to think they'd buried her father that morning. She felt a pang of guilt that she wasn't grieving, but her father had always been a difficult man to live with. Now life was returning to a different sort of normal, whatever that meant. Nothing was ever going to be the same again.

The major changes in their lives up till now had been gradual. They'd left the poky little miner's cottage after Nellie and James were married. James had inherited the factory soon after, when his father died and he had been able to offer them a much larger and more modern house.

She'd got her own room for the first time in her life and was delighted to have somewhere to study in peace. James and Daisy had been married, what was it? Seven years or thereabouts. Ben was working at the factory and her mum had remained at Dad's beck and call. At last, she could start to have a life of her own, except she was probably too old now.

'So Lizzie, have you decided what you're going to do now you've finished school? Don't know how you could have put up with it for so long.' Jenny had left her own schooling behind her

16

many years ago, when she had been just a teenager.

'I enjoyed it. But in answer to your question, I just don't know what I'm going to do. Everyone keeps on at me to decide, but I just don't know. I'm thinking of moving away somewhere for a bit. I'd really love to go to London, but I'd need to be earning before I can do that.'

'You're so brave. I'd never dare go anywhere far away from here. There's nothing to drag me away any road.' She glanced at Ben and smiled as he gave her a wave.

'You like my brother, don't you?'

Jenny blushed and lowered her eyes. She spoke softly.

'He's very good looking. And nice with it. Some blokes are too big for their own boots. Not your Ben though. Has he . . . well, has he got a girl?'

'Not that I know of. He's never mentioned anyone and I don't think he goes out that much. He's a bit shy. Just goes to the Social Club on a Friday night. Should I tell him you like him? He might ask you out one evening, if you like?'

'Oh, don't you dare. I'd be that embarrassed, I wouldn't know where to put myself.'

'Leave it to me. I'll try to test the water. See what he thinks of you. You never know, he might be feeling just as shy as you are and it's high time he was coming out of himself. For goodness sake, he's twenty-one. Our Nellie was married with a baby when she was his age and Joe and Daisy were a lot younger when they got wed.'

They continued to walk round the immaculate garden, while Ben and William were getting red-faced and rather muddy, each time the ball drifted onto the flower beds.

'I'll have to wash and change him before his father sees him,' Jenny said looking worriedly at her charge.

'Is he very strict with the little lad?'

'A bit. I think his parents were that way with him. I doubt Mr James ever really had much fun himself when he was little. It's the way things were in those days. He was sent away for schooling when he was only just eight years old and I suppose he thinks young William should have the same treatment. Him and Mrs Nellie go on about it something awful. Oops, I'm sorry. I shouldn't tattle, should I?'

'It's all right, Jenny. I shan't say owt. I thought there was something going on at tea. Our Nellie shut him up when he started to talk about it. Poor little thing. Look how he's enjoying himself with that football.'

'Nellie's good with him. She lets him play outside a bit and she plays games with him when she's home. I don't think Mr James knows much about playing with kiddies at all. I don't mean he doesn't care but . . . '

'He doesn't have any experience.'

'I really thought they'd have had another one or two kiddies.'

'I think they wanted them. Well, our Nellie did, but it just hasn't happened.

Some people are like that. I suppose we'd better go back inside. We're stopping for supper . . . dinner, I mean.'

'So I understand. I'm supposed to be helping with waiting at table.'

'Well mind you don't spill the soup down our Ben's back. He's got his best suit on. Even if his good trousers are now all muddy. Come on, you two. It's almost dark out here and it'll be dinner time soon.'

'Thank you, Ben. That was brilliant fun. Will you come and play with me again?' William asked.

'Course I will young 'un. You're shaping up into a nice little player. You'll be signed up for Stoke City before you know it.'

'Really? I don't think Father will let me play though. I've got to go to school for very many more years yet.'

'Aye, well maybe he's right. You'll have to take over the factory one of these days. You need to be educated for that, right enough.'

'Come on now, William,' Jenny

instructed. 'We need to get you cleaned up and changed for dinner. You're eating in the dining room tonight as it's a special occasion.'

'Oh, yes. My grandad got hidden away today, didn't he?'

'Buried love. He got buried,' Lizzie corrected. 'Granny is feeling sad so you'll have to be a very good boy. We're all a bit sad because we've had to say goodbye to him.'

'Why? Isn't he coming back again?'

'No. He's left us forever. It's what happens when someone gets old.'

'Will we all get old? Even me?'

'Course we will. I can remember when I was your age. Your mummy used to tell me lovely stories and draw pictures for me. Some of her pictures were made into those plates in the china cupboard.'

They reached the front door and Jenny took William's hand and went round to the back. Lizzie watched, as she and Ben went into the front.

'I'll never understand why someone

like us can go in the front door and Jenny's supposed to go round the back. We're all just the same inside, aren't we?'

'What were you and Jenny talking so hard about?' Ben asked, wiping the mud off his shoes as best as the doormat could manage.

'Oh, this and that. Why do you ask?'

'Just wondering.'

'She's a nice girl, isn't she?'

'I reckon. Not that I know her really.'

'You should ask her to go to the pictures or something with you.'

'Why would I do that?'

'Cos it's about time you were looking for a girl of your own. You can't stop at home for ever.'

'I know that. That's why me and some lads are thinking of getting a place. You saw our mum's face though, when I suggested it. Then when you started saying stuff on top of it, she looked as if she'd been kicked in the teeth.'

'Yes, well we didn't pick the best time

to say anything, either of us. She's still a bit raw after our dad going. You'd better go and tidy yourself. James won't like it if you go to the table looking like that.'

'Don't know how our Nellie stands all this dressing up and stuff.'

'She likes it. She's as bad as James these days. They always dress up you know, even when it's just the two of them. Wears her diamonds and everything.'

'She's come a long way has our sister. Practically runs her half of the factory, you know. Not that I see much of her with me being down the clay end. But she does send her designs down for me to make. Special orders and everything. Any road, I'll go and wash in the cloakroom. Make myself respectable enough for his lordship.'

'Don't be like that. He's all right really, is James. He's done us proud as a family. And you've got on all right at Cobridge's. You're getting a good wage.'

'I deserve it, what with my talents an all.'

Lizzie joined Nellie and her mother in the drawing room. They both looked relaxed and comfortable with each other's company. Lizzie would feel happier about her own future if she knew that her mother was living here at Cobridge House.

She could take life easy at last and be well looked after for her final years. She deserved it after her years of toil.

Enoch, her father, had been a difficult old man, especially the last few years since he'd retired from the mines.

His health had worsened and he had always been full of complaints. In some ways, it was something of a relief to know that he wouldn't be around, complaining about anything and everything. She blushed, hoping neither of the others could tell what she was thinking.

'You've got a bit of colour in your cheeks, Lizzie. Bit of fresh air's done you good. And I do like the way you've done your hair. Very smart.'

'Thanks, Nellie. My hair's so curly I

24

never know how to tame it. Putting it up like this means it stays tidy. I wish I had straight hair like yours. And you look so smart now you've got it bobbed.'

'Makes it easier to look after. Now then, is our Ben getting himself cleaned up? I saw him racing past the window with young William.'

'I think our Ben is a bit sweet on Jenny. And she likes him. I told him to ask her out, but I bet he won't. He's too shy by half.'

'Don't you go teasing him, my girl. He'll clam up and he's bad enough as it is.'

'I won't say a word,' Lizzie promised with a grin that suggested she meant none of it.

They sat at the table soon after half-past six. It seemed to be more of a sombre occasion as they began the formal meal. James was the perfect host, as always and despite Nan's disapproving frown, offered a good red wine with the roast beef.

Even Lizzie was given a small glass which she drank with an air of sophistication she didn't feel. In fact, she didn't like it very much, but would never have lost face by admitting it. Ben would have preferred a beer but drank the wine anyway, as it was all he was offered.

'That was a champion meal, thank you,' Ben said as he wiped round his plate. 'You really do always put on a good spread.'

'And you're always hungry,' Nan said with a frown. 'I reckon he's got hollow legs. Never a spare ounce of fat on him and he practically eats us out of house and home every day. Thanks again, you two. As always, you've done us proud. And I'll think on what you said. What's that they say? Tomorrow's the first day of the rest of your life. Such as I've got left to me.'

Life Moves On

Though Nan had taken a few days to get used to sleeping alone, strangely, she still missed the constant disruption she had been used to with Enoch's snoring and coughing.

She kept waking up to listen for it. It was difficult to accept he was no longer there after all their years of marriage. She was still thinking about her future and couldn't make the final decision to move either to somewhere smaller or to Nellie and James's house. She went down to make tea and sat in the kitchen nursing her cup as if it might somehow provide an answer.

Living with Nellie and James would mean a whole new life change. They had plenty of room at Cobridge House, but could she really live there? People always around doing everything. No more cooking or cleaning. Even her clothes would be washed for her. It sounded very tempting. But she'd always have to be on her best behaviour.

Dressing in her best every night, just to eat her supper. And what would happen when James had one of them there dinner party things? She would feel right out of place. No, living with her daughter and son-in-law wouldn't suit her at all.

'Mum? What are you doing down here so early? And who were you talking to?'

'I wasn't. I mean I must have been talking out loud. I'm thinking.'

'Still worrying about what to do? Is there some tea left?'

'In the pot. Bit stewed by now, but still drinkable. See what I mean? I couldn't come down and make a pot of tea in the morning if I felt like it. Not living at our Nellie's.'

'Course you could. They'd never mind.'

'But that Ethel and Mrs Potts and

the rest of them would all be hanging around. Couldn't have a few minutes peace like I've been used to all me life.'

'I'd be happier knowing you'd be looked after properly. This place will be much too big for you if we leave. And whatever happens, you know we shall leave one day.'

'Maybe Ben will find himself a girl and they can come and live here with me.'

'Maybe. But I think he'll want a place of his own. Oh, did I say James was supposed to have spoken to the editor of the Evening Post? I'm to go for an interview soon. I don't know if it's what I really want, but it'll be a start. And I really need to earn some money. I'm sick of being broke.'

'Oh dear, why does everything have to change all the time?'

'Good job it does if you ask me. You surely couldn't want life to be like it was when I was little. I can remember you were always really poorly and our Nellie leaving me to look after you and dad when he hurt his hand. We were always hungry and there was never any money. Then she got wed to James and everything changed. Do you think she loves him? Or did she just want to make life more comfortable?'

'Our Lizzie! Wash your mouth out. Of course she loves him. Whatever love means. They didn't have it easy when they were first wed. His parents disowned him and it was only after his father died that they went to live at Cobridge House.'

'I didn't know that. Why did he go back then? I'd have told them to get lost.'

'Someone had to save the factory. His mother was a stuck up madam. I would have loved to bring her down a peg or two!'

'Mother. Wash your mouth out,' Lizzie laughed. 'But then she died anyway, soon after the father, didn't she? Then our Nellie became the grand lady and took over. She has done well for herself though, hasn't she? She's still *our* Nellie though and she does try her best to help us all out when she can.'

'She's a good girl. And she's very clever. Like our Ben says, she practically runs the decorating and design side of things. Maybe she could give you a job at the factory.'

'What me? I can't paint or draw to save my life.'

'Maybe you could do something on the business side of things. You're good at sums and all that stuff.'

'I doubt James would let me loose on anything to do with his precious money matters. I'll see what the Evening Post offers, if anything. Look at the time. Hadn't we better give Ben a shout? It's time he was up and getting off to work.'

'I'll start his breakfast. Smell of bacon usually rouses him.'

'It's a lot better than the bread and dripping we used to have. Whatever you say about the good old days, I like it much better now.'

* * *

Once Nan had cleared out the remainder of Enoch's clothes, she felt more prepared to face the future. Several of the members of her chapel had been delighted when they received suits and shirts and all the other good stuff he had collected over the years. Much of it was scarcely worn as he was in the habit of keeping most things for *best*, even when an appropriate occasion presented.

Nellie usually gave him presents of something new when he didn't wear his good clothes to one of her events, believing he'd had nothing suitable.

The empty wardrobe seemed symbolic of her life and she decided she needed to do something about it. She tackled her son and daughter at supper one evening.

'How serious were you really about leaving home?' she asked them.

'Well, I was quite serious until you pointed out it would leave you here on your own,' Ben said. 'I didn't want to go off at this time, when you're still

32

missing my dad.'

'That's nice of you, lad. Thoughtful. What about you, Lizzie?'

'I'm not sure. I still haven't had that interview yet so I suppose I'm stopping here for a while longer. What's going on, Mum?'

'I've been trying to make my mind up. I'm seriously thinking of moving into our Nellie's place. Then if I don't like it, I'll take up the offer of a smaller house of my own. But if you two are stopping on here, then I shan't be doing owt, shall I?'

'I'd like to go, Mum,' Ben told her, 'but I don't want to upset you.'

'What happens if you do get somewhere and then you meet a nice girl? Or if one of the others you're sharing with finds someone special? You'll not want to start married life sharing with some other lads in the same house.'

'I suppose not. But when am I ever going to meet a nice girl?'

'There's always Jenny,' Lizzie piped

up. 'She's soft on you. You should have seen the look on her face when she was outside watching our Ben and William playing football. You should take her out, Ben, like I said. Hey, why don't we all go to the dance at the Town Hall on Saturday? I can ask her and you can tag along with us.'

'I can't dance. Any road, why would she go out anywhere with me?'

'Cos she likes you, daft head. All right then, take her to the pictures. You used to like the pictures when you were a lad.'

'I daren't ask her,' Ben said blushing furiously.

'I'll ask her for you if there's a problem. God, you can be thick sometimes, our Ben.'

'No need to blaspheme,' Nan snapped. 'That sort of talk is unhealthy. I don't know where you learned it.'

'Sorry, Mum. Everybody says it nowadays.'

'Not in this house, they don't. Now you can clear the table and put the kettle on. I need a cuppa.'

The two siblings cleared the table and Ben lingered in the scullery.

'Do you really think Jenny would come out with me?'

'Course she would. She'd love it. Should I ask her for you? It might have to be another night instead of Saturday cos she often has to work then.'

'All right. Go on then. There's a new Laurel and Hardy at the Regal. Ask her if she'll come with me on Saturday.'

'All right, you're on. I'll go round to Nellie's tomorrow. Now, you take the cups in. I'll mash the tea.'

Lizzie was grinning with delight the next morning. She loved matchmaking and had been instrumental in arranging several dates for her friends at school. She had never been involved with anyone herself, although several boys had asked her out.

She was determined to wait until she met the right one before she went out with anyone. Her friends had often told her she might miss the *right one* if she never went out with anyone, but she knew her mind.

She certainly wasn't going to get tied down like Nellie or her brother, Joe, however happy they might seem.

She set off soon after breakfast, knowing she'd be sure to find Jenny before she went out to do the errands. Once William had gone to school, it was usually her task to take Cook's shopping list down to the town and take the food orders to the butcher and greengrocer.

On market days, she often bought the fresh food that was brought in from the country so she would be out a while longer. Lizzie planned to accompany the maid so they could have a good old gossip. She liked to know what was really going on at her sister's big, posh house.

'So come on, what's the gossip?' she demanded as the two girls walked down the road together.

'Nothing much. Mrs Nellie is working harder than ever. I think there's something going off at the factory, but they don't say much in front of us. They're still arguing about whether little William should be sent off to school. I know the Master's booked him a place somewhere, but Mrs Nellie isn't budging on the matter. I hope he doesn't have to go away, poor little mite. Besides, it might mean the end of my job if he isn't here for me to see to.'

'I'm sure they'd keep you on. You do lots more than look after William, now he's at school all day.'

'Maybe. But I don't want to be a parlourmaid all my life.'

'Maybe you won't have to. Not if you meet a nice bloke and get wed.'

'How do I ever get to meet anyone? Even if I planned to go out, chances are they'd need me to work.'

'That's where I can help you, my dear. You like my brother, Ben, don't you?'

'Course I do. He's right good looking and nice with it. Bit shy maybe, but I like him right enough.'

'Well, he wants you to go the pictures with him. On Saturday night. What do you say?'

'Really? You're sure you're not putting him up to it?'

'Course not. He wanted to ask you himself, but he's at work and I said I'd do it.'

'Oh, I hope I don't have to work on Saturday. I haven't been told anything, so tell him yes. Yes please, I'd like that.'

'Brilliant. He'll be dead pleased. He mentioned the Regal so it won't be far.'

'Oh Lizzie, I'm that excited. What do you think I should wear?'

'Nothing too posh. It's only the pictures after all. Just be comfortable.'

'No chance of me being posh. I don't have anything posh. Don't need it. I wear my uniform all day and sometimes I don't even change at night. Depends what's going off. I've got to leave the order at the butcher's now and then it's the greengrocer. If you want to go off somewhere, I don't mind.'

'No, I expect you're going to the

market. I'll come with you. Our Joe or Daisy might be there. I can say hello.'

The two girls wandered round the market, not hurrying and enjoying a good gossip. Daisy wasn't at the usual stall so Lizzie said a polite good morning to Mrs Baines, Daisy's mother.

'Would you like to take half a dozen eggs for your mother, dear?' she offered.

'I haven't got any money with me.'

'That's all right dear. We are sort of relations after all. Have them as a gift.'

'Thank you, Mrs Baines. That's very good of you. Mum'll be very pleased.'

'Why don't you come over to see us sometime? Joe says you've finished your schooling now and you might like a bit of country air. You can stay with us in Daisy's old room, now they've got the cottage.'

'I'm not sure what I'm going to do yet, but thank you for the offer. Send my love to Joe and Daisy will you? I'd better get on now. I'm with my friend.

And thanks again for the eggs.'

She clutched the paper bag of eggs and hoped she'd manage to get them home without breaking them.

'That was nice of her, wasn't it?' Jenny said. 'You can put them in my basket for a bit 'till I start collecting stuff myself.'

'She's all right. It's her old man who's the pain. You wouldn't believe some of the stuff our Joe went through before they were wed.'

It was a pleasant morning and Lizzie had quite decided that Jenny and Ben were right for each other. She almost started planning the wedding, but said nothing. Best wait till they'd at least one date she thought with a smile.

'What are you looking so pleased about?' Jenny asked.

'Nothing. Just enjoyed this morning.'

'What, doing the errands?'

'Makes a change. I'll let you know what Ben says about meeting on Saturday. I'll come round tomorrow, anyway. I'll see you then.'

Lizzie could hardly wait for Ben to get home. He arrived covered in white clay dust, as always.

'I've got some news for you,' she burst out as soon as he came into the kitchen.

'Let me get in. I need a bath.'

'Yes I know, but don't you want to know my news?'

'Go on. Tell me. I shall get no peace 'til you do.'

'Jenny says yes. She'd love to go to the pictures with you on Saturday.'

'Really? Blinkin' heck, Sis. You did it. Crikey. She'll go with me then?'

'That's what I said. I'm seeing her tomorrow with the details.' She paused and stared at him. 'You know it's funny. Our dad used to come home black as the coal face and you come home white as snow.'

'Aye well, we're both just as mucky in our ways. Difference here is that we've got an inside bathroom. No more buckets of water out in the yard.'

'Times change.'

Satisfied with her matchmaking attempts, the next day, Lizzie turned her attention to her own future. After all her hard work in gaining an education, not forgetting Nellie's support, she felt it was important to do something that would be challenging.

She did not have the patience to be a teacher and knew she would always feel out of place if she tried to get a place at college or university. Besides, she needed to be earning some money.

It seemed working on the local paper was the only option at present that interested her. She decided there and then to go and see the Editor without waiting for James to set something up. She changed into her smartest suit, brushed her long hair back into a bun, believing it made her look older and went downstairs.

'I'm going out, Mum. Can you spare me some coppers for bus fares? I'm going to look for a job.'

'You do look nice. Where are you going?'

'Thought I'd see if the Evening Post can come up with something.'

'But I thought James was going to try and set up something?'

'Yes, well I reckon he hasn't done owt yet. I'll see if I can do something by myself.'

'Right, I see. Well good luck to you. You deserve to get on. Here you are. I'll have the change back mind, if you don't spend it all.' She handed some coins to her daughter and smiled fondly. 'I can't believe my little girl is all grown up.'

'You should be used to it now, Mum. I'm the last one of us to grow up so you've had plenty of practise.'

'Something you never get used to. But you're right. You need to think about your future and earning some money of your own. We can't go on relying on Nellie to keep us.'

'Nellie's got plenty of money. She doesn't mind. Anyway, I'll get off and see what the world of journalism can offer. Don't know when I'll be back. Ta-ra, Mum.'

'Ta-ra, ducks. Mind you're polite to the man. Don't want anything bad going back to James. He knows all the important people in the town.'

The Evening Post served a large area of North Staffordshire and was the newspaper of choice, taken by a large number of the population for their news. It was a significant building on the outskirts of Stoke itself. Lizzie braced herself and pushed open the door with a confidence she did not feel. There was a large oak desk filling an impressive space in the entrance.

'Good morning,' she said to the man behind the desk. 'I'd like to see the Editor, please.'

'Oh yes, Miss. And do you have an appointment?'

'Not exactly, but I'm sure he'll want to see me.'

'And why do you think that?'

'Because he will be certain to want me to work on the paper.'

'Sorry, miss. If you knew the number of young girls who think they want to be journalists, you wouldn't even be here.'

'And does he know how many clever, talented young girls you turn away?'

'He's very grateful that I save him from wasting a good many hours of his precious time. Now, if you want to leave your details, I'll see they are passed to the appropriate person.'

'My details?'

'References. Qualifications. Application form. Anything else you might think is relevant.'

'But I haven't brought anything like that. I was going to rely on seeing him and pleading my cause in person. My brother-in-law is a friend of his. He was supposed to be speaking to Mr what's-his-name on my account, but I thought it might be better coming straight from me.'

'I see. You'd also be surprised to know just how many friends our Mr Apperly is supposed to have. Knows the majority of the inhabitants of the Potteries I shouldn't wonder.'

45

'Well James does know him, so there. My brother-in-law is James Cobridge. Cobridge China? You must surely have heard of that.'

'Yes Miss, but if he hasn't arranged a meeting for you, I can't help you. I suggest you write in and if Mr Apperly is willing to speak to you, he'll get in touch.'

'When I do become a reporter on this paper, I shall make sure how unhelpful everyone knows you are.'

'I don't doubt it, Miss. Now if you'll excuse me, I have work to do.' He looked down at the sheaf of papers on his desk, picked up a smart looking fountain pen and began to write.

'Excuse me, but who are you?'

'I'm the sub-editor. Our receptionist is currently off sick and I'm having to stand-in 'til we can get someone else who's free to come and man the desk and let me get back to my real job.'

'I'll do it. Go on, give me a trial.'

'I'd be hung drawn and quartered if I

let some stranger do such an important job.'

'I can answer the telephone. Speak to anyone who comes in. Then you can finish your work. Looks like quite a heap of papers you've got there.'

'You've got a nerve, I'll give you that.'

Lizzie noticed a slight twitch at the corner of his mouth. The phone rang. Before he could move, she ran round the desk and picked up the handset.

'Good morning. Staffordshire Evening Post, can I help?' She listened. 'One moment please, Sir.' She looked at the row of switches. 'Can I ask who's calling? I'll see if he's available.'

She pushed the lever, hoping she could bluff the man watching her into believing she knew what to do. She had looked at the telephone system at James's factory and so did have some vague idea about how it worked.

'Mr Sellers? I have a Mr Duncan on the line for you. You're through. She put her phone down once she could hear someone speaking.'

'Impressive. But we don't need a receptionist. Not after today.'

'I don't want to be a receptionist. I want to write.'

'Can you type?'

'Er . . . not really. I have used my sister's typewriter. Well, her secretary's typewriter. But I could learn. I'm a quick leaner. I've got my advanced school certificate.'

'I see. And what name do you go by?'

'Lizzie Vale. Actually, I suppose I'm Elizabeth really, but I don't think I've ever heard anyone call me that.'

'Well, Elizabeth really Vale, you'd better fill in an application form and the next time we're taking on any staff, you'll be on our files, ready for consideration.'

'I see. And when is that likely to be?'

'That, I do not know. Could be a month. Could be six.'

Her face lost its smile.

'Oh dear, that's no good. I need a job now. Maybe I'll have to let my brother-in-law have that word with the

Editor after all. Thanks anyway.'

The man at the desk smiled. She was quite a case that one. He hated to admit it, but she was just the sort of girl they wanted to be working on the paper.

Someone with a bit of confidence and personality. He might mention it to the editor himself, in case her brother-in-law did speak up for her.

A Plan Is Hatched

'How did you get on with the job-hunting, love?' Nan asked when Lizzie returned.

'No good at all. I even answered the phone and everything. But they wouldn't let me see the Editor, not without an appointment.' Lizzie described everything that had happened.

'I expect he was busy. P'raps James will have more luck when he sees him.'

'It's all wrong though, Mum. People shouldn't have to rely on someone else's say-so all the time. It happens everywhere, doesn't it? In the potbanks, father and son, mother and daughter often work side by side. Down the pits, it's always the dad or brother who *has a word* to get someone else taken on. I'm good enough to be taken on because of my credentials.'

'You'll find something soon.'

'Maybe, but I do need to learn to type. Do you think Nellie would lend me a typewriter?'

'She might, but I think you have to go to college to learn shorthand and typing. You could be a secretary if you did that.'

'Mum,' she almost shouted. 'I don't want to be a secretary. I'm going round to our Nellie's tomorrow to ask her. It's Saturday, so she'll be at home. I can make sure Jenny's all organised for her date with Ben. I might stay on so don't worry if I'm not back for supper.'

Ben had arranged to meet his girl at the end of Nellie's road. He didn't want to knock on the door and have to face everyone who knew him.

He couldn't bear to be teased and knew that Jenny wouldn't like it either. Lizzie was to confirm it all when she went round on Saturday afternoon. Jenny waylaid her on the way on. The maid was looking distraught and had clearly been crying. Lizzie pushed her into an alcove so they could speak

51

without being overheard.

'Whatever's the matter?' she asked. 'You look awful. Aren't you well?'

'Oh, I can't believe it. They've only gone and arranged one of them dinner parties for tonight. All done at short notice. Cook's going mad and Ethel and Doris are rushing round like scalded cats. Important people in the pottery industry. Everything's got to be just so and all the best stuff's coming out.'

'Oh, I see. And that means you've got to be on duty?'

'Course it does.'

'Didn't you tell Nellie you'd got plans?'

'Well, I tried, but you know how she is. Just assumed I'd be there. I'm that disappointed and your Ben will never ask me out again.'

'Course he will. But I've got an idea. We're about the same size and your hair's the same colour as mine. If I pin mine up and put a cap over it, I could pass for you. Easy.'

'How do you mean?'

'You can go out and I'll wait at table.'

'But Mrs Potts and the others, they'll all let on.'

'It'll be too late then. We'll wait till the last minute and I'll change into your uniform, you change to go out and slip out quietly while I begin waiting on. I've watched enough times to know what to do.'

'Oh, but I couldn't. Mrs Nellie would sack me on the spot.' Jenny had gone quite pink with excitement at the plan.

'Leave her to me. I'll tell her it was all my idea and if she's busy talking, chances are she won't even notice. Ethel and Doris usually do most of the actual serving at table, don't they? You mostly fetch and carry stuff from the kitchen.

'I'll keep my head down and look the other way. Come on, say yes. Don't look so worried. You'll still have your date with Ben and I'll get valuable experience as a waitress. You just never know when it might come in useful.'

She took some persuading and raised every objection she could think of, but finally gave in. Lizzie was delighted by the whole plan. She spent the afternoon with Nellie and William, acting as calmly as she always did. She asked about the loan of a typewriter and Nellie said she would try to arrange it.

'Tell you what. You could come into the office and Clarrie might even give you some lessons.'

'That would be excellent. And when do you think James will have time to speak to the Editor of the Post?'

'Actually, I think he's one of the dinner guests this evening. He's doing a feature on the various major potteries and wanted to chat informally to one of two of the owners.'

'I see. So it's a pretty important lot coming tonight?'

'It certainly is. I should go and get ready soon. Will you help see William to bed? Jenny will be busy getting everything ready and I won't have much time myself.'

'Course I will. You'll like your Auntie Lizzie putting you to bed, won't you?'

'Will you tell me a story?' the little boy asked.

'Course I will, love. What's it to be? Pirates? Cowboys and Indians?'

'Now Lizzie, you're not to go exciting him or frightening him or he'll never go to sleep. And he has to be a specially good boy this evening. His daddy thinks it's time he went away to school but if he's good, we might persuade Daddy to let him stay at home till he's much older, mightn't we?'

'We'll be fine, won't we love?' She winked at the boy and he giggled.

'We'll be good, won't we Auntie Lizzie?'

Nellie went to get dressed for the coming evening and Jenny came to give William his tea and get him ready for bed. He was quite used to the evenings when he wasn't allowed to stay up and see his parents' guests so made no complaints. Jenny was positively shaking with nerves at the prospect of their plans.

'I've laid my share of the table. I usually do the cutlery. Mrs Potts always does the flowers and the others sort out the china. Are you really sure about this? Cos if not, you'd better go and tell your Ben I'm not coming.'

'No way am I doing that. No chance. I'm looking forward to this evening. The Editor of the Post is among the guests and I want a job with him, so it's too good a chance to miss. I can see what he's really like.'

'But you mustn't say owt. Really you mustn't. We'll be found out right away if you as much as open your mouth.'

'I know how to keep my gob shut, never fear. Now, let's get this lad of ours off to bed. I've promised him a story. Pirates, isn't it?'

'Yer, pirates.' He leapt onto the sofa, wielding an imaginary cutlass.

'William, get down immediately,' Jenny snapped. The child's face fell and he looked close to tears. 'Come on now. You're getting much too excited.'

'No story if you don't get straight to

bed. You'll get me into trouble as well,' Lizzie said pulling a sad face. William laughed and bounced up the stairs to his room.

Lizzie told him the promised story and kept it as simple as possible so he didn't get any more excited. Nellie came in to say goodnight, dressed in her finery and wearing her beautiful diamond pendant. They both kissed the little boy and left him to settle down.

'You are lucky to have such lovely things,' Lizzie said with a trace of envy, touching the diamond.

'You'll have lovely things too, one day.'

'Not if this flippin' war happens. They keep talking about it then they say it won't happen. I've heard so much about the first war and they said it could never happen again in a lifetime.'

'I can remember some of it. I was only little, but I know how awful it was when the news came out every day.'

'But it will be worse now. They've got better guns and stuff and they say aeroplanes will be used much more. I wonder if we'll get bombed up here?'

'I don't even want to think about it. Hopefully, it will be called off. They always promised us the last one was the war to end all wars. Now, I must think of something more cheerful or I'll be a terrible hostess for the evening. What are you going to do now? There may be some leftovers in the kitchen if you want to stay on. I can't ask you to join us at dinner as we're evenly balanced. Besides, James has business to discuss.'

'Don't worry about me. I'll be out of your way in good time.'

'Is everything all right, Lizzie? You look a bit strange. Has something happened to make you look sort of . . . well, excited?'

'Nothing. It was nice to spend time with you and William. He's such a lovely little lad.'

'I'm very proud of him. Now, if you'll excuse me, I need to go and check the cocktails are laid out ready.'

'Have a nice evening.'

'Thank you, dear. And I'll try to organise some typing lessons for you.'

'Thanks, Nellie. Night.'

Nellie went into the drawing room and Lizzie hovered near the kitchen door. Jenny emerged carrying a tray, which she took into the dining room. She looked terrified when she saw Lizzie.

'I've been thinking. I can't do this. It's ever so nice of you to try to help me, but I'm too frightened to leave you here in my place. Please, will you go and tell Ben I can't make it. If you explain why, I'm sure he'll understand.'

'Don't be daft. Is there much more to do in the kitchen?'

'Not really.'

'Make an excuse to go up to your room in about five minutes. I'll change into your uniform and you can sneak out of the back door. You'll just be in good time then. I'll remember everything you told me you have to do. They'll all be so busy flapping over the meal and serving, they won't notice.'

'Oh dear. All right, but I'm still dead worried.'

* * *

Everything went to plan. Jenny changed into her best dress and coat and Lizzie changed into the maid's uniform. She pinned her hair up and settled the starched cap in place.

'Perfect. Two peas in a pod. Nobody will ever notice the difference. I'll just take the trays from Doris and Ethel and none of the guests will even see me. Now, go on and have a lovely time. I'll go down first and make sure the coast's clear.'

She tiptoed down the stairs and beckoned her friend.

'I'll unlock the door at ten o'clock so make sure you're not late back. You'd better tell Ben what's happening and ask him to wait out in the road so he can walk me home. I'll make some excuse to go to your room and change out of your clothes and back into mine.

If you're needed to do anything else, you can go down to the rest of them again. Now, go on and enjoy yourself.'

The corridor to the back door was clear and she went along and practically shoved Jenny outside before turning the key in the lock. Someone was bound to check if it was locked.

Keeping her head down, she went to the kitchen and hesitated before pushing the door open. As expected, everyone was rushing around madly.

A full tray was thrust into her hands and she took it to the dining room, hoping she could work out what she was supposed to do with it.

It was a tray of starters and she wondered if she should put them out in the places or leave them on the side to serve when the guests were seated. She hoped she wasn't about to fall at the first hurdle.

She tried to remember what happened when she was a guest at the table. They came in and sat down and yes, the starters were usually in each place, ready. She set them out and hoped this was the case when it wasn't just family at the table.

'Right, you'd better all go to the toilet and wash your hands. We'll be ready to go in five minutes,' Mrs Potts, the housekeeper, instructed.

Ethel and Doris giggled as they went to the bathroom. Lizzie hung around in the dark corridor, hoping nobody noticed her. She followed them into the kitchen when they came back. Luckily the two maids were great friends and Jenny was usually left out of the giggles and chats. It was a good thing on this occasion. Lizzie knew the routine.

The two maids always served at the table and collected the dirty plates and cutlery. Jenny waited behind the screen with an empty tray to load them and take them to the kitchen.

She returned with a laden tray with the next courses, to be served by the other two. Simple. Sometimes, the others had to help when there were a number of things to be carried through.

It was all going perfectly.

At last, desserts were served and the meal was almost over. She was leaving with the tray of the last dishes, when Nellie called her.

'Jenny? Could you ask Cook for an extra jug of cream please?'

'Yes, Ma'am,' she muttered and scuttled out of the room. 'They want more cream,' she whispered and put her head down.

'You'll have to take it. Ethel and Doris are just having a bite to eat.' The cook poured cream into a jug and handed it to Lizzie. 'Well, get a plate you silly girl. Carry it on the silver tray. What's come over you?'

'Sorry.' She went through to the dining room and prayed that Nellie wouldn't notice her. Mind you, she thought, it would be a lot worse if it was James. Silently, she put the jug and plate beside Nellie and turned to leave.

'Serve our guests please, Jenny,' Nellie ordered. Lizzie smiled and took the plate to one side of the first lady she came to. She wished she could plonk the jug down and leave it to them, but the agony went on and she walked round the table.

She caught Nellie's eye and she came back to the other side of her. There was a start of recognition and a twitch at the corner of her mouth. The game was up.

Fortunately, her sister said nothing and Lizzie was able to escape from the room. Horrors. She knew she would have to face Nellie and somehow, explain things sufficiently well so that Jenny didn't get the sack.

The clock struck ten and she silently crept to open the door. The maid was waiting, white faced and shaking. Ben was standing behind her. She lifted her hand and nodded to him to wait.

'Quickly, go to your room and I'll follow you.'

Jenny rushed upstairs as quietly as possible and Lizzie was following her.

'Hang on, you,' Ethel called. 'There's coffee to be poured.'

'Need the lav,' Lizzie hissed, hoping

she sounded like Jenny.

'You'll have to wait. Come on.'

'Sorry.' She ran upstairs and into Jenny's room. The girl was waiting in her petticoat and Lizzie tore off the apron and her dress and handed it over. She tugged the cap and Jenny pinned it in place.

'I told Ethel I needed the lav. She was a bit cross when I said sorry and ran. You've got to serve the coffee, apparently. Go on. It's all been fine. Remember to lock the door after me.'

She didn't mention anything about Nellie recognising her and didn't ask how the date had gone. She would ask Ben later and call round here again tomorrow to see if any explanations were needed. Ben was waiting outside the front hedge and looking anxious.

'Our Lizzie, how could you? Poor Jenny was frightened out of her wits all evening. Can't say she took in any of the flicks. I'd have made another date with her some other time, but she said you insisted.'

'Relax Ben. It was all OK. Nellie only looked at me once and she smiled, any road. I think she thought it was quite funny. Don't think any of the others noticed at all. Jenny's there to finish off now so everything's fine. I never did get to speak to the Editor of the Post though.'

'I should hope you didn't open your gob at all.'

'No. I don't think there'll be any problems. Any road, how did you get on with Jenny?'

'It was all right, but she was too worried to say owt much really.'

'Shall you take her out again?'

'I hope so, but next time, it will be on her proper evening off.'

'That's all right then. She's ever so keen so you'll be all right there. Hope Mum's all right. Not a word to her about this evening. Except to say you had a nice time. Right?'

'You know something, our Lizzie? You're getting just as bossy as our Nellie.'

'Well that's all right then. She's a good enough one to copy, isn't she?'

They walked home and found Nan fast asleep in her armchair with the radio on.

'Wake her gently,' Lizzie whispered. 'Mum? Mum?'

'Lizzie? Where've you been? I was that worried.'

'I told you I might stay on at Nellie's. You really must get a telephone put in. Then I could have rung you and reminded you that's what I was doing. Besides, being in on your own, you need a phone in case you're taken poorly.'

'Don't make such a fuss. I've managed all this time without one.'

'Shall I put the kettle on, Mum? Make us all a nice cuppa?' Ben suggested.

'Thanks, love. That would be nice. And I dare say, you'd both like a slice of cake. There's some in the tin in the kitchen.'

'Goodo. I'm starving.' Lizzie realised

she hadn't eaten anything since lunch.

'Didn't you eat anything at Nellie's? Not like her to let you go hungry.'

'I wasn't hungry then,' she lied. 'I'll help Ben.' She joined her brother in the kitchen. 'I must have something to eat. I really am starving. I'll get some bread and cheese. Keep our mum talking while I eat it or she'll suspect there's something wrong. And not a word about this evening. You know what.'

Once she'd eaten her snack, Lizzie went to join the others. Ben was telling their mum about his evening with Jenny and avoiding any mention of Nellie.

'And do you think anything will come of this girl? You know what I mean.'

'It might. She's a lovely girl and she didn't hate me,' Ben said with a grin.

'Course she doesn't hate you. She's quite smitten with you, you know that,' Lizzie burst out. Ben blushed. 'Play your cards right and we'll be having another wedding to celebrate before long.'

'That would be something to look forward to,' Nan said enthusiastically. 'Then we just have our Lizzie to see settled and everything will be fine and dandy. Don't you know any nice lads at work that you could introduce her to?'

'I'm not thinking of settling down yet awhile, thank you very much. I want to do something with my life before I'm saddled with a family.'

'That's not a nice way to talk. We've always been a happy family, haven't we?'

'Like I said earlier, times were hard when I was little. I wouldn't want anything like that for my kids if I ever have any.'

'I don't know. You young people have some funny ideas. But whatever happens, you need to get some sort of job and soon.'

'P'raps I could be a maid or a waitress,' she said with a wicked grin at her brother.

'You? After sweating away at your education all those years. I'll have to have a word with Nellie's James and see if he can't find you a decent job.'

'We'll see. I'm going to bed now. It's late and I'm tired. See you in the morning. Night all.'

Lizzie went upstairs and lay on her bed. She really hoped that Nellie wouldn't say anything to Jenny. Not before she got there to make some sort of explanation.

An Enterprising Idea

Nan and Lizzie went to call on the Cobridge family after Sunday lunch. It had become a routine since Enoch died. It gave Nan the chance to spend time with her grandchild and catch up with Nellie.

'Have you decided what you want to do, Mum?' Nellie asked almost as soon as they arrived.

'I did think I might move on here with you for a sort of trial period. Then if we get on each other's nerves, I could take up James's offer of a smaller house. But I'll wait a bit 'til Ben knows what he's doing. He's sweet on your Jenny so maybe there'll be a wedding in the offing before too long.'

A flicker of understanding crossed Nellie's face and she glanced at Lizzie.

'I see,' she said with a slight smile.

'So, they've been walking out, have they?'

'I think so, not that anyone ever tells me anything.'

'Well, well. I'll have to be careful about settling on her evening's off, won't I?' Lizzie looked away. 'It's all right, dear. James didn't even notice. You did well, but we'll need to have a chat later.'

Nan looked puzzled.

'I don't know what on earth you're talking about. Now where's that grandson of mine? His gran wants to see him while she can.'

'I'll go and find him,' Lizzie offered. She wanted to know if Jenny had been told off and how she'd liked her brother. She needed to know if her self-appointed role as matchmaker had been successful.

'Are you really sure you don't mind if I come and live here with you? I mean to say, it's a bit much having someone around all the time.'

'Oh, Mum. We've got a whole lot of

people living in the house already. Three maids, a cook and a housekeeper for a start. You're hardly going to be a burden to us.'

'But what will happen when you have James's business friends coming for a posh meal I'd be very out of place. In fact, I'd hate it.'

'You could always eat in your room. Or with Mrs Potts. You like her, don't you?'

'I'll think about it a bit longer. I don't want you to be embarrassed, having me around.'

'Oh, Mum.' Nellie hesitated. She had to admit, her mother would hardly fit into their lives and it might prove awkward at times. But she could hardly say that to the woman who had given her life.

Her mother was looking quite old, Nellie realised. She'd had a hard life and they had been forced to scrimp and save for many years. But then, considering how ill she had been for years, she was doing rather well nowadays. It showed what good food and a life with less worries could do for someone.

'Here comes William with Lizzie. You can hear them a mile off. She's so full of energy I wonder where it all comes from.'

'Hello, my darlin' boy,' Nan said as they came into the room. The little boy ran over to her.

'Gran! Gran!' as he flung himself onto her knee. He looked guilty and caught his mother's eye. 'How are you today?' he added politely, almost giving a bow.

They smiled and relaxed as Lizzie excused herself to go and chat to Jenny.

'So, come on, tell me all about the evening,' she demanded. Jenny was tidying the nursery and playroom now that her charge had gone.

'It was nice, but I was that worried you'd be found out. Well, we'd both be found out.'

'Ben said you were worried. But did you like being with him? Did you get on well?'

74

'Ooh, he's lovely. I hope I wasn't too boring for him. Do you think he'll ever ask me out again?'

'I'm sure he will. Anyway, I'll make certain of it. Next time, we'll make sure you have a proper evening off. It was very mean of our Nellie to cancel it at the last minute like that.'

'It's always part of the deal. We get our evening off unless we're wanted for something. She always let's us have another evening if it gets cancelled.'

'Don't know how you put up with it. Wouldn't do for me. I don't think I'll become a waitress after all.'

'You are funny, Lizzie. Did you get to see the chap you wanted to see?'

'Not really. I know which one he was, but of course I couldn't actually speak to him. I just hope James says something soon.'

They chatted for a while longer until Lizzie thought she'd better excuse herself in case Nellie became even more suspicious. It was a pleasant enough afternoon, though nothing was actually resolved regarding her mother's future. The fact that Lizzie and Ben were still living with her, meant that no decision could be reached for a while.

Lizzie did her best to avoid being left alone with Nellie to avoid the threatened 'chat'. The longer it was left, the less likely it was to be a problem.

Nellie did agree to her sister spending some time in the factory, ostensibly to learn to type but in her mind, Nellie was forming a plan to get Lizzie to put together a new brochure to show off their ware.

She felt her sister might bring a new angle to the rather staid document that had been existing since James's father's time.

After a week of struggling, Lizzie was beginning to understand the typing techniques that Clarrie had shown her. It was a heavy old typewriter and the girl's wrists ached with the unaccustomed movements, but she was proud of what she had achieved.

'Well done, Lizzie,' Nellie said when

she showed her the first perfect sheet she had produced. 'I've had a bit of an idea about something you could do to earn some money. I'd like to employ you to produce a new brochure for the factory. I'll get some new photographs taken and you can write the words to go with them. Look, this is the one we've been using forever, it seems to me.'

'You really do need something new. This has got things in it you haven't been making for ages. Sounds a good idea. I'd really enjoy that and it's the start of my career in writing. Thanks, Nellie. And I'd be glad to earn a bit of money.'

'Instead of waiting at tables for no pay, you mean?'

'Erm . . . well yes. Look, I'm sorry about that, but Jenny was so looking forward to her first date with our Ben. They're both so shy, it took me all my time to get them fixed up. Then you went and arranged that dinner party.'

'Jenny knows the rules. She'll have an evening off at another time.'

'But it was all arranged. And you said yourself, I did well. And James didn't even notice.'

Nellie frowned at her.

'Maybe no harm was done, but it was very wrong of Jenny to ask you.'

'Of course it wasn't Jenny's idea. Not at all. It was all mine. In fact, if you want the truth, she was too nervous to really enjoy herself. She thought you might find out and give her the sack.'

'Well, don't let it happen again. I haven't said anything to Jenny so we'll let it go for now.'

When her sister had left the room, Nellie smiled. Typical Lizzie. She was always trying to organise everyone. It was probably just like she had done herself, when she was a teenager and the main breadwinner in the family.

Lizzie worked hard for the next few days and collected samples together for photographs to be taken. They booked a local photographer to come and spend the day at the factory.

Lizzie took charge of him and asked

him to include a number of pictures of the people who worked there, as well as the china itself. She also asked him to take a picture of the outside of the building, showing the huge bottle shaped kilns.

Her ideas had moved away from something simple to a much more informative brochure which would show potential customers something of the processes involved in manufacturing the goods. When James was finally shown the completed booklet, he was impressed.

'This is an excellent piece of work, Lizzie, but I'm afraid it will be far too expensive to produce in printed form. We have to print large quantities to send out all over the world and the whole thing, good though it is, it won't bring enough customers to merit the cost of it all. I've got to think of the outlay.'

'But James,' Lizzie wailed, 'that's just so old fashioned. You need to show the world what you are capable of doing.

Let me take this to the printers and get estimates. You don't know how much it would cost just by looking at it.'

Her brother-in-law smiled at her enthusiasm.

'I have a fairly good idea. Very well, you can try, but don't be disappointed. Printers have to make money as well you know. They won't do this amount of work for less than a properly workable fee.'

'Leave it to me. I'll find someone who will print it. What's the most I can spend?'

He named a figure that she felt was acceptable and she set off with her work and the photographs in a folder. She went into one of the largest printing companies and displayed the work.

'For Cobridge's, you say?' She nodded to the man behind the desk. 'This will be expensive. Photographs always cost dearly. You can leave it with me and I'll work something out.'

'How long will that take?'

'Next week, sometime.'

'I'm afraid that is quite unacceptable. I need a prompt answer today. I'll have to try somewhere else. Mr Cobridge expects an immediate answer.' Lizzie sounded considerably braver than she felt.

'Oh, does he now? Can't say he's ever given us his business before.'

'Perhaps because you don't give fast enough service,' she answered pertly.

'Hand it over again. I'll take a look at it and give you an answer shortly.'

'That's more like it. I do have a budget so we'll see if you meet it. I'll take a seat over here.'

'Give me an idea of what you're willing to pay.'

'Certainly not. I'll see what you come up with and see if we can agree to it.'

The printer looked at the young girl standing before him. Who was she to speak so confidently and to be negotiating something so important?

'Can I ask what your position is with the company?'

'I'm on the creative side. My sister is

the chief designer.'

'I see. And would that be Mrs Nellie Cobridge, by any chance?'

'Well, yes. You know her?'

'By reputation. If you want an answer any time soon, you'd best let me get on with working it out.'

Lizzie sat nervously waiting. She looked through the windows at the large machines crashing through their tasks. The workers looked grubby with hands that were as black as her miner father's had been. There was a smell to the place. Different to the china factory, but still distinctive.

After some time, he handed her a piece of paper with a series of figures scrawled on it. She looked him in the eye and collected her papers and photographs together.

'I'm sorry, but that's exactly double the amount I'm authorised to pay.'

'I might do it for a bit less for a large order. But certainly not half the price per brochure.'

'I'm sorry to hear that. Thank you for

your time. I'll try elsewhere.'

'You can try, but you'll not get anything much better than my offer.'

'We shall see.'

'My offer stands for the rest of this week only. I can do it at that price while there's a gap in my orders. After that, the price will be higher and you'll have to wait longer.'

'And so will you. I'm sorry if you have a gap in your work, but I'm not paying that price.'

'I'm surprised you're even thinking of printing a new brochure at this time. From what I hear, the factory's not having much of a time of it at present.'

'Really?' Lizzie was somewhat taken aback. She had heard nothing about the company having difficulties. No more than James ever moaned about orders being slow.

'Difficult times for all of 'em I guess.'

'Well, you don't need to repeat your thoughts to anyone else regarding the Cobridge works. The order books are in good shape. Thank you for your time. Good day.'

She walked out, head held high. The printer smiled to himself. Stuck up little prig. Who did she think she was? Whatever she said about her brother-in-law's company, he knew what he knew and nothing was as good as she might think. They were in the same boat as most of the companies around.

Lizzie went to several printers, but it was the same story each time. The cost of printing the new brochure was way more money than James had said he would pay. Perhaps he had been right in trying to quash her optimism.

'What if we cut down on the number of photographs?' she asked in the last printing company.

'Well, it would certainly reduce the price, but it would be a pity. Whoever put this together has made a nice job of it.'

'I know. It gives a real feel of the company. It's my first job too. I might as well not have bothered if we can't afford to print it.'

This final print shop was a fairly new one and the owner was quite young. He liked the pretty girl with her direct gaze. Maybe she was worth a gamble.

'I expect the company has a number of printing jobs? Headed notepaper, business cards and the likes?'

'Oh, but of course.' Lizzie sensed an offer.

'Well, if you could guarantee more work would come our way, I'll take this on. As it stands and for the price you named.'

'Really? Oh that's wonderful. Thank you so much, Mr . . . er what's your name?'

'Charles Swift. Most people call me Charlie. And you are?'

'Lizzie. Lizzie Vale. It's my brother-in-law who owns the factory and my sister is Head Of Design. She's married to James. And my brother, Ben, he's one of their main throwers. You know, potters' wheels and making vases and stuff.'

'So, I have the complete family history, do I?'

'Oh, no. There are more of us.' She paused and noticed the man smiling. 'I'm sorry. I do go on a bit.'

'Not at all. I'm fascinated. Do you know, I've never actually been round the Cobridge potbank. Looking at these photographs though, it's something I should do.'

'Come round our place. I'm sure they won't mind, especially if you're producing the new brochures. I'll have a word with James and see what we can arrange. It might have to be soon though cos I'm not going to be there much longer. I'm hoping to be a journalist.'

'I see. Ambitious.'

'For a girl, you mean?'

'For anyone. Well now. Let's complete the paperwork and get down to business. I'll have to ask for a deposit before I start, of course.'

'Oh, well I haven't got anything with me.'

'Perhaps you could drop it round tomorrow?'

'Or you could come to visit the factory and collect it? Then I could see about giving you a tour while you're there?' She had wondered how to organise it, knowing she been somewhat impulsive on her offer. But she rather liked this earnest young man.

'Then I'll see you tomorrow. Ten o'clock suit?'

She nodded. Very much so, she thought. Any time she might spend with this young man would suit her well.

A Chance To Impress

Lizzie left her precious folder with Charlie Swift and positively skipped along the pavement. Then she remembered she was a young lady of eighteen years and trying to be responsible for a large expenditure in her brother-in-law's company.

All the same, she had succeeded where James had thought it would be impossible. What a nice person Charlie seemed. She hoped that nobody would mind if he was shown round the factory. She rushed straight up to James's office and knocked on the door.

'I did it, James. I've got a thousand brochures for the price you agreed. He's a lovely chap. Very nice indeed. You should get all your printing done with him. Charles Swift. He's a new company and willing to offer good prices to get going.'

'You mean you've actually placed the order?' James looked worried.

'Well yes. He's coming here tomorrow to collect the deposit and I said I'd show him round the factory. He was so interested when he saw the pictures. I hope that's OK?'

James sighed.

'I suppose so. You were right. The old brochures were certainly past their best and your ideas are excellent. How old is your printer friend, by the way?'

'Twenty-something, I guess.'

'And good looking, I presume?' There was a twinkle in his eye as he suspected there was more than just printing this particular young pair were interested in.

'Haven't thought about it,' Lizzie replied, a fiery blush spreading across her cheeks.

'I'll see him when he arrives and write a cheque for the deposit. And Lizzie, well done. I admire your enterprise.' If her charms had got such a good price for the printing work, why should he complain?

'Thanks, James. Oh yes, one of the printers I called on, said that Cobridge's is having difficulties. That's not true, is it?'

James looked down.

'Of course not, Lizzie. Now if there's nothing else, I do have a lot of work to do.'

'Yes, of course. Thanks.' She turned to leave and hesitated, there was something in James's eyes that suggested he was being economical with the truth.

It would be a disaster for all of them if the company went under. There were tales all round the Potteries of well known names having hard times. She went along to Nellie's office, determined to ask her for the truth.

'Nonsense,' was her sister response. 'We're doing fine. Order books are as full as ever. But the whole country is on alert with this threat of war coming again.'

* * *

Lizzie dressed more carefully than usual the next day before going into the factory, ostensibly to continue her typing lessons. She told the lodge keeper that she was expecting a visitor and he was to be shown up to Mr James's office.

'And you'll need to call me as well. In fact, if you call Mrs Nellie's secretary, I'll come down right away and show him up myself.'

'I see. Someone special, is it?' George, the lodge keeper asked. 'I remember your sister having that same twinkle in her eye when she were a young 'un.'

'Really, George, I don't know what you could possibly mean.'

'You're looking very smart today, anyhow. You going to be working here full-time now?'

'Oh, I don't think so. I still want to be a journalist, if I can.'

'Good luck to you then, Miss. I'll let

you know when your visitor arrives.'

'Thanks, George. See you later.'

She was on pins for most of the morning. Perhaps Charlie Swift had thought better of it and wasn't coming after all. She tried to convince herself that they had never fixed a set time and he would come when he wasn't busy. Perhaps she hadn't given George the proper name and he'd been shown to James's office.

'Whatever's up with you this morning?' Clarrie asked. 'You just don't seem to be settling down to anything. Now, have you done those typing exercises I showed you?'

'Course I have. Loads of times.' The phone rang and she jumped up to answer it. He was here. Charlie had arrived at the factory gates. 'My visitor's here,' she called as she rushed out of the room. The secretary shook her head as she settled back to work.

'Charlie, you came. I was worried you'd decided not to print our brochures after all.'

'Miss Vale. Nice to see you again.' He held out his hand to shake her own, but she was totally flummoxed and held out the wrong hand.

'Sorry,' she mumbled. 'Come along, I'll show you to my brother's office. He was pleased at the deal and says he'll write a cheque right away. Write . . . right. Not wrong.' *Shut up*, she told herself. *You're babbling like an idiot.*

'I've brought an invoice and some samples of the various printing jobs I can do. I hope we really can do more business in the future.'

'I hope so too. Come up here. This is where the main offices are.' She knocked on James's door and went in. 'This is Charles Swift, James. James Cobridge, Mr Swift. Shall I wait outside?'

'You can stay, Lizzie. It is your deal, after all. Pleased to meet you, Mr Swift.'

'Please call me Charlie. I hope we shall be working together for a long time. Now, here is my invoice and the quote as agreed with your sister-in-law. I require a ten percent deposit on agreement of the quote and I guarantee to have the job completed by the end of the month.'

'That all sounds excellent. Thank you. I'm pleased and somewhat surprised by your quote. Very competitive.'

'Well, I'm just starting out on my own. My father ran the business for a number of years, but he's been forced to retire through ill-health. I'm looking for new customers wherever I can.'

'That all sounds fine. I'll see the quality of your work and hopefully, if it meets out standards, we shall be able to place further orders with you.'

'That's what I hoped and why I'm prepared to give you such a good deal.'

Once the business was concluded, Lizzie began her tour of the factory. She introduced Ben, working on his potters' wheel and they went on through the various departments until they finally reached Nellie's office overlooking the decorating shop.

'I don't know why they always call them shops. Tradition I suppose.'

'It's all fascinating. Where does the designing happen? I mean, it's well known your sister is in charge of the designs. Do you think I might meet her?'

'I'm not sure what she's doing at the moment. I'll see if it's all right. They don't usually let visitors into her studio place. All a bit hush-hush.'

'I can understand that. It's just that my own work involves quite a lot of art work. I'm really interested to see the design process in the pottery world.'

'I'm sure it will be fine. I'd better ask though.' She knocked at the door and went in. 'Nellie, I've got Charlie Swift with me. He's the new printer we're taking on to do the brochures. He'd like to meet you if you've got time. He's really lovely.'

'I see. Like that is it?' Nellie grinned at her little sister's enthusiasm.

'I don't know what you mean.'

'Oh, Lizzie, you look like the cat that

got the cream. Big grin on your face. All dressed up to look smart. Just be careful though, love. You're very young and well, inexperienced. With men, I mean.'

'Yes, big sister. Having two brothers and a brother-in-law, oh and a nephew, means I've hardly spoken to any men.'

'You know very well what I mean. Hadn't you better show him in, so I can get a proper look at him?'

'Yes, of course. Thanks.' Still somewhat pink in the cheeks, Lizzie opened the door and invited the young man to step into Nellie's studio. 'This is Charlie. Charlie Swift. He doesn't like to be called Charles, even though that's his proper name.'

'Mrs Cobridge. It's a pleasure and honour to meet you. Your name is a legend in the Potteries.'

'Well, thank you for the compliment. I'm pleased to meet you too.' She looked into the blue eyes and liked what she saw. He was certainly good looking and seemed to have very nice manners. She could see why Lizzie was smitten.

'Can I ask where you get your inspiration, Mrs Cobridge? Your designs are so well known.'

'I'm not really sure. I suppose I look at shapes and the china and also some of what is currently available in the shops and try to find something new. One thing leads to another. What's your interest?'

'Well, I often have to produce designs, logos for companies and so on. People regularly come to us to ask for headed notepaper, for example. It's always good to be able to produce something individual for them and I need to produce a quick design as a basis for the work. Occasionally, they know exactly what they want so that's a different matter entirely.'

Lizzie sat on the edge of a desk, fascinated by what he was saying. He had a very slight Potteries accent, but nothing like as strong as most of the locals.

She watched his hands as he was talking. Expressive hands that moved constantly, as if he was trying to shape his words at the same time.

He was quite fair haired and had bright blue eyes that were always darting round, taking in his surroundings.

'Exactly what sort of printing capacity do you have at your offices?'

'I can do simple colour printing of course, but it is fairly labour intensive so becomes more expensive. It's a fairly basic set up. I shall expand as soon as finances allow.

'I can do large posters of course and everything down to business cards. I'm just very pleased to be able to produce your brochure for you. It won't make me much profit, if any at all. But if I do a good enough job, I shall hope for much more work in future.'

'Wise man.'

'So, are these the designs for your next line? What will it be used for?'

'It's a dinner service. Altering the

sizes potentially makes it suitable for a complete range. Tea sets and a range of serving dishes too. Popular as wedding presents. People like to buy items separately to cut down costs.

'It's a fairly new idea, as previously the services were always sold as complete sets. Replacements for breakages are available, but usually have to be special orders and thus, are usually more expensive. This way, the cost is always the same. Some people want sets of eight or ten so it all becomes much more flexible.'

'That sounds amazing. Most innovative. They are all very attractive. Well, I shouldn't take up any more of your time. Thank you so much for letting me see them.'

'A pleasure. Perhaps you'd like to come for tea one Sunday, with Lizzie?'

Charlie looked surprised and somewhat shocked. As for Lizzie, she went quite red. 'Sorry. Have I got it wrong?'

'Nellie,' Lizzie chastised. 'Charlie hardly knows any of us.'

'I apologise. I assumed you two were either walking out or at least planning to see more of each other.'

'Thank you for the invitation. I was going to ask Lizzie if she would be kind enough to spare me some more of her time one day, but I hadn't quite arrived at that point yet.'

'Well, the offer's there. I'm sure Lizzie will let me know in good time if you do decide to take it up.'

'Thank you. And thank you again for showing me your new designs.'

The pair went out and Nellie smiled to herself. She may have precipitated something, but she wasn't worried by it. It was high time Lizzie showed some interest in a boyfriend and high time she grew up. Charlie seemed a nice enough chap to start with.

'I'm sorry about my sister,' she said as they walked down the corridor.

She felt hugely embarrassed and wanted this tour to end as quickly as possible. How could Nellie have done this to her?

'I take it as a compliment,' Charlie replied. 'But I really wanted to ask if we could meet one Sunday? A walk in the park perhaps? It would be wonderful to get to know you. We could even go to the flicks one evening. Or perhaps you enjoy dancing?'

'I've never been to a dance and only once or twice to the pictures. With one of my brothers. You know, Ben. You met him down the clay end.'

'Of course. Excuse me asking, but it seems strange that someone so pretty as you hasn't been to a dance. Is there some reason?'

'I stopped on at school. I've been studying. I got my advanced school certificate with honours.'

'So why aren't you trying for college or university? A lot of girls are doing so nowadays.'

'I don't want to spend any more time on book learning. I want to do something with my life. I'm eighteen already and as you point out, I haven't even been to a dance.'

'I see. Well Lizzie Vale, once we know each other a bit better, I hope I'll be the first one to take you to a dance. So, what do you say? Shall we meet on Sunday next and take a walk in the park?'

'All right then. Where shall I meet you? I don't know where you live.'

'I live with my parents, over the shop. How about you?'

'Three roads down from the factory. Briton Street. But I don't want you coming to the house. They'll be teasing me rotten. Supposing we meet at the end of our road and then we can walk up to the park. If that suits.'

'Suits me very well. Shall we say two-thirty?'

'I'll look forward to it. I'd better show you out now.'

'Thank you again for the tour. And thank you for the introduction to the company. It was truly my lucky day when you walked into the print shop yesterday.'

'Mine too,' she said, her cheeks turning pink once more.

News For Lizzie

'So, did you arrange to see him again?' Nellie asked when her sister came back to her office.

'What if I did?'

'Good. I'd be pleased to see you spreading your wings a bit and he seems like a really nice chap. But you must be careful. Has Mum talked to you about things? You know, men and everything?'

'Course she hasn't. It's our mum you're talking about. But I'm not daft, our Nellie.'

'I know, but it isn't a matter of learning from books. Men aren't the same as us.'

'I should hope not. Men need everything doing for them. Slippers warming by the fire and food on the table. Oh and clean shirts and socks.'

'Oh dear, Lizzie. We shall have to

have a proper talk and soon.'

Lizzie burst out laughing.

'Course I know men are different. I was joking. Laugh? Ha ha?'

'All the same. You do need to know what's what. Just be careful. A lot of young girls get themselves into trouble thinking they know everything when they don't.'

'Just cos you're an old married woman, our Nellie, you've forgotten what it's like to be eighteen and possibly, even to have fallen in love.'

'Now you are worrying me. You haven't a clue what love is. And you've only just met the lad. Though he's possibly a bit old to call him a lad. Just be careful, love. And I certainly haven't forgotten what it's like to be eighteen. From what I remember of it, it was all work and no play. I was feeding the family when Dad was out of work. Yes, well, enough of this reminiscing. I need to get back to work. I've got mountains to do before I can go home.'

'I'm going home now. I haven't got

anything else to do here. Besides, I need to find something to wear for Sunday.'

'Oh Lizzie, you're incorrigible. But you can bring him for tea after your walk.'

'We'll see. Bye, sister dear.'

* * *

There was a letter waiting for her when she got home. Her mother was most curious to know why someone should have been writing to her youngest daughter. Lizzie tore it open and gave a whoop of delight.

'At last my life is beginning properly. I've got an interview with the Evening Post and I've got a sort of gentleman friend. Good old James. He must have put in a good word for me at last. I'd better go round to Nellie's and use their phone. I'm supposed to let him know if I can attend. Ten o'clock a week on Friday.'

'Well done, love. You go and tell them you'll be there, all right.' Nan was delighted that the girl was finally thinking about a proper job.

'We should get a phone put in here. It would save such a lot of bother.'

'Don't you start. You'd never be off it chatting to your friends.' But Lizzie wasn't listening. She had bounced off to get her coat and hat and she slammed the door as she rushed out.

Nan sat down again. What had Lizzie said? She'd got a sort of gentleman friend.

What on earth did she mean by that? She was far too young to be having gentlemen friends.

She gave a sigh as she realised her baby daughter wasn't too young at all. She had been pregnant with Nellie when she was eighteen. And Joe was practically married at the same age. Nellie wasn't that much older either. Where had the years gone?

'Oh, Enoch,' she murmured. 'I don't think I'll be long behind you.'

Lizzie rang the doorbell at Nellie and James's house. She almost walked straight in, but she knew that would not be approved. Jenny came to the door.

'Lizzie. Hello, come in.'

'How are you? Got over your date yet?'

'Has Ben said anything about seeing me again? Only I've got tomorrow night off. I was sort of hoping we might go somewhere. Make up for the last disaster.'

'I'll let him know. I came to use the telephone. I've got an interview with Mr Apperly. You know, the Evening Post. I have to confirm it. And Jenny, I've met someone. A man. He's ever so lovely. And I'm seeing him on Sunday.'

'That's nice for you. Look, I'd better go or Mrs Potts will be on at me. I'm supposed to be sorting out William's tea. He'll be back from school in a minute and he's always starving.'

'Right. Well I'll go and use the telephone. And I promise I'll have a word with Ben later on today.'

Her arrangements made, Lizzie decided to stay on and see her nephew. She went up to the nursery and shared his tea.

'So, have your mummy and daddy decided about your school in the autumn?'

'I don't know. Daddy says I'm going to his old school and Mummy wants me to stay here.'

'And what does William think?'

'I don't know. But it doesn't matter what I think, does it? I'd quite like to meet the other boys, but I don't want to go away from home and you and Jenny and everyone.'

'Maybe you should tell that to your daddy?'

'He doesn't want to listen to me. He's always too busy and sometimes he's quite cross lately. You won't tell him I said that, will you, Auntie Lizzie?'

'Course not, darling boy. I'll never say anything unless you want me to. Now, eat up that sandwich or I'll be in trouble for talking to you too much.'

'I hate sandwiches. Banana ones anyway.'

'I hate them too. Not that I've ever had one.'

'How do you know if you hate something then?'

'It's just something you say. Hate is a bit of a strong thing to say. We should really say we don't like something unless it's something very serious.'

'Banana sandwiches are quite serious.'

Jenny arrived to see if tea was finished. She noticed the rejected banana sandwich and quickly ate it herself, giving both of them a broad grin.

★ ★ ★

Sunday couldn't come quickly enough for Lizzie. She spent most of the morning trying on a large percentage of her wardrobe. It was so important to get it right. She needed to be smart and stylish, but not overdressed.

Nellie had given her several outfits that she had decided were unsuitable for someone of her own age. She had a reputation to keep up and didn't want to be accused of mutton dressed as lamb. Lizzie had hung them away carefully, waiting for the opportunity to wear them. She eventually settled for a dark turquoise dress and with a long jacket.

She had a cloche hat in a similar colour, another hand-me-down from Nellie, and which she believed completed her outfit perfectly. She went down to get her mother's approval before lunch so she had plenty of time to change her mind if Nan didn't like it. Ben was in the living room and whistled when he saw her.

'What's the big occasion? You look as if you're going to a wedding or something.'

'Oh dear, is it too posh for a walk in the park.'

'I'd say so. You'll get it all muddy when you kick the football round.'

'Oh, for heaven's sake. I'm not six any more. I don't kick footballs anywhere. I hope you didn't treat Jenny like that when you went out with her.'

'Course not. I'm only teasing, our Lizzie. You look lovely. Very smart. Very like Nellie used to look before she got older. Any road, I had a nice time with Jenny. Thanks again for letting me know she had an evening off. She's a lovely girl. I'm seeing her again next week. I think she might be the one for me, you know.'

'Oh Ben, that's lovely. I'm so pleased. So I take it you've cancelled your plans to get a place of your own? With the other lads, I mean.'

'Well, for the time being. Any road up, I didn't think our mum wanted to be left here on her own.'

'She won't be. If I leave home, I expect she'll go and live with Nellie and James. They were talking about it the other day. I'll go and change out of this lot. You do think it will be all right, really, don't you?'

'I dunno. No use asking me that sort of thing.'

'Well, would you be proud or ashamed to be seen with me?'

111

'You're my sister for goodness sake. Why would I want to be seen with you whatever you were wearing?'

'Oh men. You're a hopeless breed. I'll ask Mum and then I'll go and change. If I have to start deciding all over again, I'll go barmy.'

'You should be like me. I only have one outfit for best, one for very best and me work clothes. Easy.'

'Like I said. You're a hopeless breed.'

She left him grinning as he read the sports page of the Sunday paper. She hung her clothes carefully and put on her everyday things again. She so much wanted to impress Charlie.

She'd never walked out with a man before and wanted him to see her as a sophisticated young woman who knew her way about. If Ben was a bit more forthcoming, she would have liked to ask him more about how she should behave.

Once upon a time she could have asked Nellie, but she was much too grand to ask such simple things. She bit her lip and frowned.

She had been too much of a loner for too long. Her school friends, if she could even call them that, had teased her about being a bookworm and not going out with the boys. She may have organised Jenny and Ben to get together, but she hadn't a clue about her own life.

What if Charlie tried to hold her hand? Was that being too forward? Would he think she didn't like him if she refused? Why was it all so difficult?

'Lizzie? Come and help with the dinner,' Nan called. 'I don't know what you're doing up there, but I could do with a bit of help.'

'Coming,' she shouted back. She would just have to play it by ear this afternoon, she decided.

By two fifteen, Lizzie was dressed. She had settled for her good brown coat with a pale pink blouse and brown skirt beneath it. It looked smart, but not too dressy.

Her mother had finally suggested

that her other outfit was a bit too much for a simple walk. She was nervous, but tried not to show it. After all, Charlie was just a young man and nobody special. Not yet, at least.

If anyone had been able to see inside her mind, they might have been concerned that she was building him into the most handsome prince in the world, with her as his favoured princess. Distant wedding bells accompanied them as they strolled hand in hand.

'I'd best be off now,' she said at last. 'I may see you at our Nellie's later, but don't worry if I don't come. Not sure whether Charlie will really want to go there for tea.'

'Bye, love. Have a nice time and make sure you behave properly.'

'Course I will,' she replied with a grin. 'If I only I knew what properly was supposed to mean.'

'Lizzie,' Nan called after her, but her daughter swung off along the road, ready to meet her new friend.

A Serious Romance

Dressed in a dark suit and stiff collar, Charlie was waiting at the end of the road. He smiled as she approached him and stepped forward, his hand held out.

'I wasn't sure if you'd still want to meet me,' he said as he shook her hand.

'Course I did. Want to meet you, I mean. Why wouldn't I? I've been looking forward to it.'

'Good. So have I. In fact, I've been thinking about you ever since we met last week. You're a very pretty young lady.'

'Thank you, Charlie. You're not half bad yourself. Oops, I shouldn't have said that, should I? How can a man be pretty? I meant good looking of course.'

'I'm flattered. Look, I really don't mind what you say to me. I hope we can be friends and that you will be able to be honest with me at all times.'

'It's just that . . . well, you'll think I'm silly, but I haven't been out with anyone before. The only men I've known are my family. I went to an all girls school of course and well, I never actually met anyone who wanted to go out with me so I'm not sure what I should say or not say.'

'Oh Lizzie, you're lovely. Come on. Let's get to the park and if you like, I'll get a rowing boat and we can go on the lake. Then we can go to the pavilion and have ourselves some tea. Unless you have other plans?'

'That all sounds wonderful. I said that I, or we might go to our Nellie's, but I also said not to worry if we didn't.'

'I don't want to cause you any problems.'

'Oh, you won't. I go round to their place quite often enough. They won't miss me for once.'

They walked on the paths between formal flower beds. It was colourful all the year round and even in autumn still managed to have a good show of dahlias, chrysanthemums and attractive leaves.

Lizzie was looking at everything with new eyes and noticing that even the flowers seemed more colourful than she had ever noticed before. They reached the lake where they hired out rowing skiffs. Large, cumbersome vessels that were popular with all the young people at weekends. Several were occupied by rowdy young men who had probably spent too long in the public houses at lunch time.

'I'm not sure it's a good idea to go out there with all that lot messing about,' Lizzie said doubtfully. 'I can really see what my mother means about the evils of drink. They are behaving quite badly. Shall we forget the lake for now? What do you think?'

'Maybe another time would be best. I'm afraid we'd both get wet the way they are splashing around.'

'And you're wearing your good suit. Maybe we should come again on a different day when it's less crowded.'

'What would you like to do now then?' Charlie asked her.

'We can walk round the top path and then, well, is it too early for that tea you mentioned?'

'Why not? Let's have a bit more of a walk now and then we'll go for tea before it gets too crowded.'

The pavilion overlooked the lake and was always popular with families, especially at weekends. It wasn't terribly smart with green painted ironwork supporting a glass panelled roof which was covered in leaves and general debris, letting in very little light. But, they provided a good pot of tea and fancy cakes.

They went inside and Lizzie sat at a table near the window while Charlie joined the queue at the counter. The table still had cups and saucers from the last customers and the whole place smelled of tea and sweet cakes.

There was no waitress service and the ladies who worked there put everything onto trays for each customer to carry to the table. There was one lady who cleared the tables as people left, but she clearly wasn't keeping up with demand. Lizzie stacked the dirty dishes onto a tray and was about to take it to the counter herself, as Charlie arrived back.

He balanced the tray on the corner and signalled to the waitress to come and clear. Grumpily, she came over muttering that she only had one pair of hands. She wiped the table with a grubby cloth which merely served to spread the spilled tea into a wider puddle.

'Mrs Potts would never allow that,' Lizzie giggled. 'But, this is hardly Cobridge House, is it?'

'Oh, I'm sorry. Mrs Potts? I expect you're used to everything being a much better standard than this. We can go to your sister's for tea if you'd prefer it.'

'Not at all. I shouldn't have said anything. It was just a comment. Mrs Potts is the housekeeper and she's a stickler for everything being just so. She's very nice really, but woe betide you if you get anything slightly wrong. And anyway, this is all lovely. Those cakes look very tempting. I love shop made cakes. We hardly ever have them though.'

'You sound as if you know exactly what it's like if Mrs Potts disapproves of something.'

'Oh, I do.' She told him about her efforts as a waitress when Jenny had a date with Ben. Charlie was highly amused and took her hand and kissed it as he laughed. Lizzie froze at the strange reaction his simple gesture had on her.

'You are quite a determined character, aren't you?' he said.

'You have to be if you're going to get on. Like when I came to you with the printing job. I tried loads of places before I found you. I'm very glad I did. Find you, I mean.'

She released her hand from Charlie's, blushing furiously as she did so. She felt as if she should preserve the spot where his lips had touched it and knew she would never forget her first date.

'Now, which of these would you like?' He held out the plate with four different cakes on it. 'Two each I thought might do it, but I can fetch something else if you'd prefer.'

'Can I have that cream one? It looks scrummy.'

'I don't suppose it's real cream, but help yourself. I expect you're used to real cream at all times.'

'Not really. We're not that posh, you know. My sister happened to marry the boss of the company. But up 'til then, we were dead poor. Scruffy little house down Cross Street and short of food most of the time I was growing up.'

After she had regaled him with tales of her childhood, she paused.

'Tell me about yourself. I've talked the hind legs off a donkey this afternoon.'

'Nothing much to tell. You know most of it from what I said before. My dad ran the business and then became ill so I took it over. I'm pretty boring really.'

The waitress came over to ask if they had finished.

'Only I need to wash the cups and stuff and they want the tray back.'

'I'm sorry. We've been sitting here for much too long.' Lizzie smiled sweetly at the girl, who sniffed and glared as she stacked the tray noisily. Charlie reached into his pocket and gave her a couple of coins as a tip.

'Thank you,' he said to her. She glanced round to see if anyone had noticed and stuffed them in her pocket.

'Ta,' she said. 'But you'd better go or they'll only moan at me for not telling you.'

Stifling a giggle, the pair rose from the table and went back into the now somewhat chilly air. Charlie took her arm and they walked along the paths towards the main gates as if they had known each other for months.

'I wanted to thank you for giving me

a chance to do the work for Cobridge's.'

'Yes, well make sure you do a good job or my neck will be on the line. I don't really work for them you know. In fact, I've got an interview at the Evening Post on Friday. I'm going to be a journalist.'

'Good for you. They don't take on many girls as journalists though. You sure it's not a typist they're after? Or someone to make tea?'

'They'd better not be. I make lousy tea. All the same, I'll have to make it very clear what I want to do.' She frowned.

The letter had said nothing about the actual job. Merely, it asked would she attend an interview. She shouldn't get too excited.

All too soon, she and Charlie reached the end of her street. Lizzie couldn't ask him to the house, as her mother and brother would both be at Nellie's house as usual, on a Sunday. All the same, she didn't want the afternoon to end.

'I've really enjoyed chatting to you,' Charlie said.

'So have I.'

'Can we do it again sometime? I mean, will you go out with me again? Maybe you'd like to go dancing on Saturday evening?'

'Oh yes. That would be great. But what will I wear? I mean, what do girls wear at these dances?'

'I've simply no idea. Perhaps you'd rather do something else? Flicks maybe?'

'That might be best for now.'

'Actually, there's a film on next week I really wanted to see. *You Can't Take It With You*. It's won awards and everything. I think you might like it. And we can celebrate you getting that job at the Post.'

'Huh, if I do. I'm keeping my fingers crossed. But, yes please, I'd love to go to the flicks with you on Saturday.'

'That's great. Shall I meet you here or come to the house?'

'Actually, you should come to the house. My mum will want to meet you.

She likes to know where I am and who I'm with.'

'Thank you. I'll come at six-thirty, if that's OK. That will give us time for a word or two and still make it to the cinema on time.'

'I can't wait. Well, I'd better go in now. Thank you for tea and a lovely afternoon.'

'Thank you. I've had a good time.' Awkwardly, he took her hand and shook it. He leaned towards as if he was going to kiss her, but he withdrew. It wasn't done to kiss on a first date and certainly not in the street where anyone could see them.

Lizzie blushed, sensing what he had been about to do. She desperately wanted him to kiss her, but she knew it might have been wrong.

Mrs-next-door would have been round like a shot to tell her mother about her daughter's disgusting behaviour. Perhaps in the darkness of the picture house . . . She had heard other girls talking about missing large chunks of films when they had been with their men friends.

'Thanks again, Charlie. See you next week.'

She let herself in to the dark house and poked the fire back into life. It was almost six o'clock and she wondered if her mother would be coming home soon or staying on at Nellie's for supper. She went up to her room and changed out of her best things.

It was too late for her to go to Nellie's so she sat by the fire and thought about her afternoon and Charlie. He was so lovely. Everything she could want in a man friend. He was good looking. Nice blond hair, neatly trimmed. Just a bit taller than her, a nice height for kissing she giggled.

She imagined reaching up to his rather sensuous mouth and wondered how it would feel. Goodness, how pathetic she was. Eighteen years old and had never kissed a boy.

She blushed, glad there was nobody

else around to see her. *Time you grew up, my girl,* she told herself.

* * *

Lizzie went into the factory every day the following week, determined to improve her typing skills, by Friday if possible. She tried timing herself to see how many words she could type in a minute.

The results convinced her it was a matter best left out of any discussion. When she typed quickly, she made far too many errors. Corrections were a nightmare, using a strange piece of rubbery substance and then trying to line up the paper again to type over it. Clarrie told her that this would never be accepted for any important documents such as letters or invoices. Even worse if a carbon paper was used to make a second copy as it wasted expensive materials.

'It would be so good if you could just make another copy without all that messing about. Every time I use carbon paper it sort of slips and then makes a black smudge. I wonder if I'll ever get it right.'

'Why didn't you learn typing at school? That's where I learned it. Our teacher used to stand calling out the beats and we had to type to music when we'd been doing it for a bit. Wagner or some such. A march I think it was supposed to be. *Dum, dum, dum, dum te dum.* But it did get us typing, I suppose. Some of us did shorthand as well, but I went to evening classes to learn that properly.'

'I wasn't allowed to take it at school. It was only the commercial pupils who did typing. Shame really cos it would have been much more use to me than learning Latin.'

'Blimey, can you speak Latin?'

'Not really speak it. But I can understand some of it. And it makes me realise where some of our words came from.'

By the time Thursday came, Lizzie

was a bundle of nerves. She had consulted Nellie about what to wear, what to say and how to behave generally. Though Nellie had rarely been for an interview herself, she did have a good idea of what a potential employer would look for. After a long diatribe of dos and don'ts, she gave up.

'Just be yourself, Lizzie. That's what's important. If you are polite and answer his questions, you can't go wrong. And wear something smart, but not showy. And for goodness sake, tie back your mop of hair. Pin it up or something. It looks dreadful today.'

'I washed it last night and it got all bushy and horrible. I've decided to have it all cut off and then I won't have to worry.'

'Oh no, you don't. Trimmed maybe, but you mustn't have it cut short. It wouldn't suit you.'

'You don't have to live underneath it. Anyway, wish me luck for tomorrow.'

'Of course I do, dear. But you mustn't hold too much store by this. If you don't get the job, there will be plenty more chances. Best of luck. Get a good night's sleep so you're ready for it.'

'Sleep? I doubt I'll get more than twenty winks. Thanks anyway.'

'Come and tell me how you get on, won't you?'

'Course. Have a nice evening.'

She plagued her mother all evening. Was her best white blouse clean and ironed? Should she press her skirt again? How should she look when she smiled?

'For goodness sake, girl. Settle down and listen to the radio. Take your mind off things. Or go and read one of your books.'

'Newspaper. I should be reading this evening's paper. Where is it?'

'Ben's got it in his room, I expect. You know what he's like with his sports pages.'

'I need it. I need to know what's going on in our world. Tell him, Mum. He won't give it up for me. He'll do it if you tell him.'

At nine-thirty the following day, almost half-an-hour before her appointed interview, Lizzie was walking up the steps to the Evening Post building. The large hallway was familiar and she walked to the large reception desk and smiled at the woman behind it.

'Good morning. I'm Lizzie Vale. I have an interview with Mr Apperly at ten o'clock.'

'I'm afraid Mr Apperly has been called away. You'll be seeing his deputy, Mr Guest.'

'Oh, but I thought . . . '

'Take a seat will you. Someone will come to collect you when he's ready for you.'

Lizzie was fuming inside. After all this, she was only about to see the deputy. She wondered if it would be the man she had met before when he was standing in for the receptionist.

All in good time, she would know. She sat twisting the envelope containing her certificates and a letter of reference written by James. She had also filled in a form provided by the newspaper with her interview letter.

It seemed that James had indeed organised the interview for her as usually, this all had to be completed before anyone was invited for an interview.

'Miss Vale? Please come this way.' A young man had crossed reception to lead her through to the offices. He showed her into Mr Guest's office.

'Ah, Miss Vale. Mr Apperly sends his apologies, but he has been called away. We met before, didn't we? I believe we shared receptionist duties.' He smiled and gestured towards a seat in front of the desk.

'Yes, indeed. I answered the telephone for you.'

'You want to be a journalist, I understand.' Lizzie nodded. 'You must understand that there is huge competition for such a role. We do take a very few young ladies, but most of our staff are men. Because of the nature of reporting news, ladies are not always able to venture into some places.'

'But in this age surely that isn't the case? I mean to say, women have the vote, have just as good an education as any boy and often get better qualifications. I have brought my certificates along for you to see and to prove I'm right.'

She took out the documents and handed them to Mr Guest. He scanned them quickly and smiled and nodded.

'Very commendable. What I can offer you is basically a secretarial post, but with opportunities for advancement to a wider role in future. Now, you were learning to type? How is that going?'

'I can type. I'm not the fastest in the world, but I am accurate.'

'And shorthand?'

'Erm, I can learn.'

'So you can't take shorthand at present?'

Lizzie pressed her lips together. Should she be honest or try to tell a white lie? She decided on the former.

'No. But bear in mind, I was not

really looking for secretarial work.'

'Reporters need shorthand too. How else do you make proper notes at council meetings and such?'

'You're right. I never thought of that. OK, I'll learn shorthand as soon as possible.'

'That's very good of you, Miss Vale.' Lizzie thought she'd blown her chances with the slightly flippant reply. But he was smiling. 'Thank you for your time. I'll let you know as soon as possible. We have other applicants to see, but it won't be a long wait. I'm assuming you will take the position if offered it?'

'I think so. If it will give me chances to become a reporter.'

'I think I can safely say so. You're clearly very keen and you have good qualifications, if not exactly at typing and shorthand. I shall discuss it with Mr Apperly on his return and we'll write to you with the outcome.'

'Thank you, Mr Guest. I look forward to hearing from you.' Her smile belied the tumult of feelings inside.

She felt angry at being interviewed by someone less important than Mr Apperly, especially after James's intervention on her behalf.

Worse than that, she was not even being considered as a reporter and was only offered the possibility of becoming one if she succeeded as a secretary. She knew very well that she was not nearly good enough for that. But she had nothing else on the horizon so perhaps she needed to give it a shot, assuming she was offered a job at all.

★ ★ ★

'Maybe you should think about doing something different altogether,' her mother suggested the next day when they walked round to Cobridge House to report on her interview.

'We all have to start at the bottom and work our way up,' Nellie told her.

'Like James did you mean?' Lizzie retorted.

'Actually, he did. He began at the

bottom and learned all the different processes so he knew exactly what was required when he did take over the company.'

'But he always knew he'd get to the top eventually, even if he made a mess of something on the way.'

'It was never certain, but maybe there is some truth in what you're saying. So, the answer is don't make a mess of anything on the way up. I had my moments don't forget.'

'Haven't been offered anything yet.'

'At least you've got your date this evening to look forward to,' Nan reminded her.

'Yes, but Charlie said we were going to celebrate my job only I haven't got one. What's he going to think about me? A failure.'

'For heavens sake, Lizzie. You might have a job. You don't know yet. Who knows what will happen?'

'I'll see what I've got to wear to go out with Charlie.'

She spent the rest of the morning

rummaging through her wardrobe. Everything seemed dull and dreary or totally unsuitable.

Once she was earning some money, she would go and buy a whole lot of different clothes. New shoes, hats and handbags to match. She couldn't wait. Nellie had paid her some cash for creating the brochure, but it wasn't nearly enough to buy all the things she wanted.

Besides, she felt she ought to pay something to her mother towards her keep. She finally decided on her outfit for the evening and came down in a more cheerful mood.

'I've been trying to persuade our Ben to do a bit of tidying in the garden. It's a right mess with all the dead flowers and things. Your dad would have hated to see the way it's gone to ruin.'

'And will he? Ben, I mean?'

'Says he's going out to the football. Then he's taking Jenny out again. They're going to the picture house.'

'Well I hope they're not going to the

same one as us.'

'Why not? Be nice for you all to be together.'

'Oh, Mum. I hardly know Charlie and I certainly don't want big brother keeping his beady eye on us.'

'I can't think why that's a problem. I don't want you getting up to anything, our Lizzie. Now peel the potatoes for me. I'm making lobby for dinner.'

'Oh, lovely.' The traditional Potteries stew was one of her favourite meals. The steak and kidney had been cooking slowly in the oven over the top of the combination grate since the night before. The mix of vegetables was added and cooked slowly so everything mixed in the stock and gradually thickened it. 'Are we having dumplings with it?'

'I expect so,' Nan agreed. 'I've got some nice fresh suet taken from round the kidneys. Be a shame to waste it.'

They worked together and soon the pan was simmering gently on the stove, making the wonderful smell that pervaded the whole house. Ben came down from his room.

'Something smells good. What time will it be ready?'

'One o'clock as usual.'

'Don't make it any later or I'll be late for the match. I won't have time to eat later cos I'm meeting Jenny at half-past six. We're going to see something Jenny wants to see. *You Can't Take It With You* or some such.'

'You would be. That's where we're going.'

'Well just you make sure you keep your nose out of my business. I don't want my little sister prying on me all evening.' Nan and Lizzie both burst out laughing. Ben stared. 'What's so funny?'

'I just said the exact same thing to our mum. I don't want my big brother sticking his nose in my business all evening.'

'It's a big place. Make sure you sit on the opposite side. Any road, just make sure you behave yourself. Maybe I'd best sit near you so I can keep my beady eye on you. You're not much more than a child.'

'Our Ben, I'll kill you if you come anywhere near me.'

'Don't worry. Jenny will have all my attention, thank you.' They both grinned and promised not to spy on each other.

Promptly at six-thirty, there was a knock on the front door.

'That'll be Charlie,' Lizzie said, excitement making her rather loud. She showed him into the sitting room and he went to shake hands with her mother.

'Nice to meet you, Mrs Vale. Don't worry, I'll look after her.'

'Pleased to meet you Mr . . . I'm sorry. I don't think Lizzie told me your name.'

'It's Swift, but I'd like it if you called me Charlie.'

They made polite conversation for a few minutes and impatiently, Lizzie interrupted.

140

'If we don't go now, we won't even get into the pictures. Our Ben left hours ago.'

'Enjoy yourselves and behave.' Lizzie treated her mother to one of her most angry glares. 'And look out for Ben and Jenny.'

As it happened, neither couple saw the other 'til they were coming out of the picture house. Ben had his arm round Jenny's shoulders and she was looking somewhat flushed.

Charlie had behaved like the perfect gentleman, despite Lizzie's attempts to put her hand so close to his arm that he could have taken it and held it very easily at any time. But she had enjoyed the film enormously. She had to introduce Jenny to Charlie as they all walked out together.

'You know my brother, Ben, and this is Jenny, his girlfriend. This is Charlie, Jenny.'

They all shook hands and walked back into the main street.

'We're just going for a drink at the

Potters,' Ben told them. 'You can come with us if you want.'

'Would you like to, Lizzie?' Charlie asked somewhat doubtfully.

'Why not?' She didn't want the evening to end, even if she did hope for some time alone with Charlie. She and Jenny both had lemonade and the men had pints of bitter.

'Isn't that Jimmy Stewart just fantastic?' Jenny said. 'He's so good looking. No wonder Jean Arthur fell for him.'

'It was a bit like when our Nellie fell for her James. His parents were furious and Mrs Cobridge was just like Jimmy's mother in the film. Really snobbish and tried her best to split them up.'

'So there's some truth in fiction after all,' Charlie suggested.

'I suppose there must be. But they all came through and lived happily ever after. Like our Nellie.' Ben smiled at Jenny and took her hand gently. She blushed but looked very happy.

'Still a lot of hard work though, keeping everyone cheerful,' Lizzie remarked.

'Well, we'd best be going. I expect you're taking Jenny home so we'll be walking the other way.'

'Where do you live, Jenny?' Charlie asked.

'At Mrs Nellie's. I'm the nursemaid to little William. For as long as he's there at least. They're still arguing about where he'll go to school. Mrs Nellie has won so far and he's still staying at the local prep school for now.'

'Well, it's been lovely to meet you both properly.' Charlie shook Ben's hand.

'Without me being covered in clay, you mean. Look after my little sister. I'm sure we'll meet again. Cheerio then.'

'Bye. Take care.' Charlie shook hands once more and took Lizzie's arm to walk her back home.

'Thanks for this evening, Charlie. I've had a really nice time.'

'Thank you. I've enjoyed it too. Nice girl, Jenny, isn't she?'

'Yes. Very nice. Our Ben is quite

smitten. Thinks she's the one for him.'
Why did she say that? Lizzie wondered.
Did she feel a smack of jealousy?

'That's nice. Sounds like another
happy ending. Now, which is the
quickest way back to your place?'

'Had enough of me already, have
you?'

'Not at all,' he grinned. 'I was going
to suggest we went the other way.'
Happily, she put both hands on his arm
and he took the one and kissed it
gently. 'Can I kiss you, Lizzie? Properly,
I mean?'

'Thought you'd never ask.' She
pulled him away from the street lights,
against the park hedge and put her
arms round his neck. He leaned down
and lifted her chin to bring her lips
closer to his own.

She closed her eyes and waited. His
mouth was soft against hers. She felt a
delicious sensation run right through
her, making her tummy feel quite
shivery inside. She might have worried
about how you were supposed to kiss a

man at one time, but it was all very natural when it happened.

'Oh Lizzie, you're gorgeous. I don't know where you learned to kiss like that . . . in fact, I don't want to know.'

'It all came naturally. In fact, you might like to know, you're the first person I have ever kissed. Except for the family and they don't count, do they?'

'Certainly not. I'm very flattered to be the first. And I think I should take you home right away. Otherwise, we could be standing here for quite some time and your mother would never let me take you out again.'

'I don't want it to end. Our first proper date.'

'We'll go out again very soon. We could go for another walk in the park tomorrow, if you like.'

'Really? Oh, yes please. Then we could go back to our Nellie's for tea if you could stand it.'

'But we haven't been invited.'

'Oh, that won't matter. Mum can tell

her we're coming. We always go round on Sunday afternoons. Mum likes to see William and it's the only day Nellie's home really. They've got a cook who always makes plenty of tea.'

'I'd like that. If you're sure I won't be intruding on the family.'

'Course not. Anyway, they all want to meet you. Make sure they know who I'm walking out with. I hope you won't mind meeting them all. There's quite a lot of us if everyone goes at the same time.'

'I've met some of you already so I'm sure I can cope.'

They reached her street and he gave her a quick peck on the cheek as he left her.

'See you tomorrow. Two-thirty, here?'

'Of course. Sleep well. I don't think I will.'

'Why ever not?'

'Why do you think? I'm still feeling all warm inside after that kiss.'

'Let's hope it's the first of many,' he said softly. 'Good night, Lizzie.'

She reached the door and looked back to see he was waiting for her to get safely home. He raised a hand and walked away round the corner. Her mother was waiting in the sitting room.

'You're late. The film must have ended ages ago.'

'We met up with Ben and Jenny and went for a drink.'

'You did what?'

'Went for a lemonade. It's all right.'

'I don't hold with young girls going into public houses. It's just not the done thing. I hope you won't be seeing him again if that's the sort of thing he does.' She tutted away angrily while Lizzie cursed herself for mentioning it in the first place.

'Is Ben back?'

'Not yet. I don't know where he can be.'

'He was walking Jenny back.'

'Well I hope she won't be in trouble for being late. Do you want anything before you go up?'

'Wouldn't mind a cuppa if you'd like one.'

'All right, if you like. I've done nothing but drink cups of tea all evening. I was that worried about you.'

'Oh, Mum, I'm a big girl now. I'll go and put the kettle on. Oh and we're taking up Nellie's invite for tea tomorrow. Will you tell her when you go round? We're going to walk in the park first. So, you'll all get a chance to meet Charlie.'

Suspicious Behaviour

It was drizzling the next day so the walk in the park was cut short. Lizzie and Charlie arrived at Cobridge House somewhat early for tea. Nan was chatting to Nellie and playing with William as they went into the drawing room.

'You've met Charlie, Nellie and my mum and this young rascal is my nephew, William.'

'Pleased to meet you Mrs Vale. Hello again, Mrs Cobridge. William.' The child looked up shyly and then stood and shook hands formally. He grinned and sat on the floor again with his model cars.

'You may call me Nellie when we're away from work. Not when I'm in the office of course, but I shall call you Mr Swift when we meet for business.'

'Thank you. That's kind of you. I

hope it's all right for me to be here.'

'Of course. The family always get together on a Sunday. Ben's somewhere around. I expect he's chatting to Jenny, if Mrs Potts permits. I leave all that to her to manage.'

'It's a lovely house. Is that all Cobridge china?' he asked, looking at the huge glass fronted cabinets lining the walls.

'Indeed. Samples of every line going back for years. From the very beginning. You can look at it if you're interested.'

'Thank you. I'd love that.'

He and Nellie became engrossed in discussion for the next half hour. Lizzie sauntered over and listened to her sister. She was impressed with her knowledge and stories she was telling about different pieces and designs. She began to think about the local interest there might be and thought about possible articles she could write for the paper.

A plan was forming in her head. Even

if she didn't get a job on the Evening Post, perhaps she could write some articles and send them in. She could even use a man's name to get them published if there was this prejudice against females. She listened more to what Nellie was saying and made plans to ask questions later and with permission, to set down her ideas on paper. She could get stories from some of the other factories as well and possibly use James's name to get an entry to them.

'I'm sorry, I've been neglecting you,' Charlie said to Lizzie. 'But it's all so fascinating, hearing your stories and seeing the pieces together. Thank you, Nellie. I've really enjoyed my tour through Cobridge history. And seeing your new designs the other day, well it completes the picture. I loved those patterns you showed me. Very special.'

'Yes, well they're all top secret at present. There are competitors who want to copy them and produce them for the mass market. You know the sort of cheap earthenware stuff that comes on the market stalls.'

'A bit like these fashions that people copy from the best clothes designers.'

'Exactly that. Now, I'd better ring for tea. I thought we'd use the dining room as there are more of us. Save balancing things on knees.'

Ethel, the head parlour maid came in.

'We're ready for tea when you're ready. In the dining room, please.'

'Cook said as you'd want it in there. Ben said there may be extras.'

'That's right, Ethel. And tell Mr James when it's ready. He's working in his office, as usual.'

'Right missus. It'll take us a minute or two as we haven't set it up in the dining room. If Jenny can drag herself away from your Ben, she might even help out a bit.'

'It must be difficult for you having your own brother courting one of your maids,' Charlie suggested when Ethel left the room.

'Not really. No doubt Lizzie has told

you of our family history with this household. Nothing surprises me nowadays.'

'She's told me a little, but not a great deal. I gathered Mr Cobridge had a problem with his parents when you and he were married. Only because of the film we saw last night and Jenny and Lizzie were discussing it afterwards.'

'We always manage, eventually. Things are not all as formal as they once were. Well, most of the time.'

By the end of the afternoon, Charlie had made a big hit with all the family. He was polite and courteous at all times and even James had a favourable impression of the young man.

'I'll look forward to seeing the proofs of our new brochure when they're done. Send them to Lizzie first and I'll see them when she's corrected them.'

'I certainly will, sir. I hope to have them ready during this week. I hope we can print more things for you in future. Oh, I'm sorry. This is business and should not be a subject for a social occasion.'

'Quite right,' Nellie replied a trifle sharply. 'But you can tell us about your family. Have you any brothers or sisters?'

'No. I'm an only one. Dad's not well so he's retired and left me to manage the business. He still keeps an interest though and always asks to see the books and wants to know everything that's going on. I'm hoping to expand, like I was saying the other day, Nellie.'

'Indeed. Now, if everyone's had enough to eat, shall we move back to the drawing room?'

'I think we'd best be getting home,' Nan said. 'Ben, Lizzie, are you ready?'

'I suppose so,' Lizzie said as she glanced at Charlie, hoping he might suggest something different.

'I'll walk you home,' he offered. Lizzie brightened.

'It's still raining, Mum,' Nellie said. 'I'll run you home in the car, save you getting wet. Jenny will see to William.'

'I'll walk back with Charlie, thanks,' Lizzie announced. 'You've got an umbrella to lend me, I'm sure.' They all smiled at the girl. She was clearly besotted with her new man friend.

'Just behave yourself, little sister,' Ben told her with a big grin on his face. 'I'm just going to say goodbye to Jenny. When's her next evening off, Nellie?'

'I'm not sure. Mrs Potts organises that. You can ask her if you want.'

Ben shot off and went to the kitchen. He returned a few minutes later with a smile on his face. Evidently, he had arranged his next date with Jenny and went out with his mother and sister to the car.

'You didn't mind walking with me, did you?' Lizzie asked her escort.

'I was very glad you suggested it. Though it does mean you'll get a bit wet. On the other hand, we can get nice and close so we both get shelter under the umbrella. But don't forget it's still daylight and it is a Sunday.'

'What difference does that make?'

'One is suppose to be circumspect on a Sunday.'

'Rubbish. Mum went to chapel this morning so I'm sure she'll have said a prayer for all of us.'

'Don't you go to chapel, then?'

'Sometimes. I do go on a few Sundays, just to keep Mum company. Ben never goes now and my dad didn't hold with it too often. Christmas and Easter were his days to go. How about you?'

'I used to go to the church school so I always went to church. I don't go any more, but that's because I just got out of the habit. Once I started work, I sort of ran out of time. I have to do quite a lot for my parents.'

They walked along the roads, taking the longest route so that the walk was extended, despite the rain. For Lizzie, she felt the large umbrella over the two of them, provided them with a little world of their own. It was as if they were secluded and hidden from everyone else.

'So, what do you plan to do if you don't get this job at the Post?'

'I don't really think I will get it. It's mostly just secretarial and I'm not good enough for that. I'm thinking of writing some articles on the pottery industry and seeing if the paper will take them. Sort of freelance. I'm going to use a pseudonym as well so they don't realise I'm a girl. What shall I call myself?' Charlie laughed.

'You're quite a case, aren't you? If women hadn't got the vote already, I can see you'd have been a suffragette. You should call yourself something a bit upmarket. Giles or something. And use a local place name. Giles Trentham. How's that?'

'I like it. I might do it anyway, whether or not I get a job. I can start with a piece on Cobridge's. The people who work there and what it's really like.'

'And there's the new Wedgewood factory out at Barlaston. Everything really modern and green fields all around it. It's all electric I gather with no smokey old bottle kilns. And there's a new station for the trains to stop for the workers and to carry the products away.'

'You seem to know an awful lot about it.'

'I like to know what's going on. I have a number of contacts with the other companies in the area. I'm building up our business so I visit some of the factories to see the buyers there.'

'So you've been round china factories before, have you?' He nodded. 'I thought from what you were saying that Cobridge's was a first.'

'They're all different. I mostly just go to the office and meet whoever's in charge of printing orders. There isn't someone like you to show me round at any of them.'

'There's only one me anywhere in the world,' she chided.

'Only room enough for one of you,' he said squeezing her arm. 'I'm glad enough about that. Now, I think this is your street. Shall we arrange to go out again soon?'

'Yes, please. Do you fancy seeing that film they showed a trailer for?'

'If you'd like to. Next Saturday then?'

'All right. You can come to the house to collect me if you like. Now you've met everyone, there's no reason not to.'

'I'll be there. Six-thirty again?'

'Fine. Now, do I get a goodbye kiss or are you going to be all stuffy about it being a Sunday and not quite fully dark yet?'

'You're incorrigible, Lizzie Vale. But come here. If we hide beneath the umbrella, nobody will see us.' He leaned down to kiss her mouth and she closed her eyes.

The umbrella handle slipped and the whole thing slid over, bumping then on their heads. 'That wasn't exactly successful, was it?' They both laughed and she took the umbrella and collapsed it, shaking off the raindrops.

'You could take it with you and give it back later,' she offered.

'It's practically stopped raining now so I'll be fine. Bye.'

'Bye, Charlie. I've enjoyed today.' She watched as he rounded the corner and then went inside. Ben was looking at the paper and Nan was stoking up the fire.

'It's got quite chilly. Getting right back-endish, isn't it?' Lizzie smiled at the old saying her mother used every year she could remember, as autumn chilled the air. 'Charlie gone home all right?'

'Yes, thanks. I'm seeing him again next Saturday night. Flicks again. Right, I'm going to change out of my good clothes. Are we having another cuppa? I'm feeling right parky.'

'You shouldn't stand around in the street so long,' Ben teased her.

'Quiet you. So when are you seeing the lovely Jenny again?'

'Keep your nose out. Soon enough.'

'Don't tell me then. She'll soon tell me when I see her next.' She ran up the stairs two at a time and changed into her old shirt and a jumper. She must do something about her wardrobe very soon if Charlie wasn't going to think she had only a couple of things to wear.

Nellie's things were all a bit too formal and much too posh to wear for the pictures. Perhaps her mum would make her some things if she got some material. Nan always used to make clothes for the two girls when they were little. Worth thinking about anyway.

★　★　★

Each morning for the next few days, Lizzie was up and waiting for the postman to call. By Thursday, she had convinced herself that she wasn't going to get a job offer and began to plan her articles.

She still went into the factory each day so she could keep practising her typing and to get ideas for her article.

On Thursday morning, the proofs for the brochure were delivered. She rushed down to the gatehouse, hoping to see Charlie, but he had used a delivery boy to bring them. She went through them carefully and corrected a couple of errors, but on the whole, she was delighted with the look of them.

She showed them to Nellie, who sent her to James to show him.

'First rate job. Well done, Lizzie. And your young man has made an excellent job of them. I'm very pleased with the way you've tackled this job and I think we can probably find a permanent place for you somewhere in the company. If you'd like it of course.'

'Thanks very much, James, but I really still want to be a journalist. But I could do with earning something in the meantime. Would you mind if I write an article on Cobridge's? Just on spec sort of thing. If I can sell it to the paper, it might be a way in for me.'

'I don't mind, but I'd want to see it first. Just in case you mention something that may be sensitive. Not for the public to read, you understand.'

'Fair enough, but I can't think what

you mean. Like I said the other week, someone mentioned rumours about problems with the factory. They weren't true, were they? I know you said there was nothing to worry about but . . . '

'Lizzie, rumours cause unnecessary trouble. Don't listen to them. And if you do produce an article, make sure it's a very positive one. I don't want any of those rumours spreading.'

She stared hard at her brother-in-law's face. He was avoiding looking at her directly. Maybe there was something in it after all and he wouldn't admit it. Somehow, she needed to corner Nellie on her own and ask what was really going on.

'OK, James. I'll be so positive that people will be queueing up to buy every single thing you make.'

'No need to go overboard. Just make sure you show it to me before you send it anywhere.'

'Thanks, James. I will. Can I say something?'

'Depends what it is.'

'Well, I know it isn't really my business, but I don't think you should send William away to some posh school. He's only a little boy and he needs his family around him. And have you ever asked him what he wants?'

'Of course not. It's not his decision and naturally, he would say he wants to stay at home. It's all he knows. He'll have a great time at his prep school with other boys.'

'But he's only little. I think it's cruel. And I didn't do so badly at the state school, did I?'

'I suppose Nellie's put you up to this?'

'Course she hasn't. I've just listened to what William says.'

'Well, as you said, it has nothing to do with you and my mind is made up. It didn't harm me.'

'That's a matter of opinion. Sorry, I'll go now.'

James stared at the door as she left his office. Cheeky young madam. He frowned though. She was quite right about certain things.

The orders were distinctly down on previous years and there might have to be cuts on the work force if things didn't improve rapidly. Competition was growing as factories were modernising. Changes to the methods of firing the china were coming in.

Electricity and gas and tunnel kilns were being put in the bigger factories. Perhaps it was time to think more about joining with other companies to install these expensive items to share costs. So much was hanging on the new lines Nellie was producing.

As for the school thing with William, was he really being unreasonable? He remembered the first time he went away from home. He had cried endlessly, but he'd always managed to keep it hidden. He'd written the obligatory letter home each Sunday and as instructed by his teachers, always said good thing about his days.

The one time he had mentioned being unhappy, the teacher had torn up the letter, insisting he wrote another during what should have been his play time. He had even contemplated running away but when another boy had done so, there had been severe repercussions and he did not have the courage to face his father's wrath. Maybe he should think again, but it would mean losing face.

Nellie was discussing the final samples of the new line with Vera, the decorating manager, when Lizzie got back to her office.

'They look nice,' she said.

'I hope the rest of the world think so. We need some new orders. Who are you going to put on painting these?'

'There are two or three good girls I'd thought of. Two from your old bench when you were still painting and I thought I'd give Mary Wiggins a try. She's a good girl and willing to learn. The usual gilders will do the banding of course.'

'OK, thanks Vera. Good work.' The woman left the office and Nellie turned back to her sister. 'Was he pleased with the result?'

'I think so. Yes, he said well done. Can I ask you something?' Nellie nodded. 'There are some rumours flying round that Cobridge's is in some sort of trouble. James denies it, but he wouldn't look me in the eye.'

'I don't know where you've heard it, but we're not in trouble, exactly. We do need to keep the order books filled but that's nothing new. There is much more competition around and some new production methods are making the competition stiffer than ever. We will need to look at improving our own methods soon. Now, was there anything else?'

'I stuck my oar in about the school thing for William. I said he didn't want to go away. I'm sorry. James looked quite cross, but I don't think he ever listens to anyone and the poor little boy is really fretting about being sent away.'

'I can imagine that didn't go down

well. Did he say anything about a job for you?'

'Well yes, but that was before I opened my big gob. I sort of said no thanks as I still want to be a journalist. I could do with some cash though. My wardrobe is in a very bad way.'

'Now you've got a young man, you need more things, I suppose?'

'Well, partly that. But if I do get a job, I've hardly got anything suitable to go out in everyday.'

'I'll see what I can do. I've got a few things that might suit you. Things I don't need any more or that I think are a bit too young for me, now I'm getting on a bit. And you'll get a fee for doing the work on the brochure.'

'Thanks, Nellie. You've always been a good sister. I thought I might go round to Charlie's now and take the corrections. He'll be able to make a start on printing then, won't he?'

'Good idea.'

Lizzie walked briskly to the printers. It was chilly and rain threatened. She pushed open the shop door and set bells jangling. Charlie came from the back, wearing a brown coat and an apron, wiping his hands on an already blackened cloth.

'Lizzie. What a surprise. I sent the proofs round to the factory this morning.'

'Yes, I know. I've got them here. There are only a couple of corrections, otherwise a perfect job. They're very pleased with them. I've shown them to Nellie and James and they both like them very much. I came round right away so you can make a start on the printing as soon as you're ready.'

'That's good news. And I'm glad they're pleased.'

'Are you terribly busy?'

'Well, yes, I am. Why do you ask?'

'It's nearly lunch time. I wondered if we could get something to eat?'

'I haven't really got time. I'm sorry. I have someone coming to see me at any minute I thought it was him when you arrived.'

'Oh well. It was just an idea. It'll be sandwiches as usual, I suppose.'

'I'll get on with your job as soon as possible. And I'll see you on Saturday. Look forward to it. Now, you'll have to excuse me. Sorry. I'm really sorry.'

'It's all right. But I'd like to watch how you print things sometime. In return for me giving you a trip round our factory.'

'Of course. One day soon. But not now. I really am much too busy.' He came round the counter and held open the door for her. 'Bye, Lizzie. See you soon.'

'Right. Thanks.' She went into the street wondering why he was so anxious to be rid of her. There was a man approaching, someone who looked vaguely familiar. He looked at her without speaking and continued as far as Swift Printers.

She watched as he went inside and then she crossed over the road, to see what was happening. She stood against the wall so she wouldn't be seen.

The two men were talking animatedly and then, much to her surprise, the stranger picked up her proof file and flicked through it. How dare he? And why wasn't Charlie stopping him?

Who was he and why did he look familiar?

Now Charlie was sketching something on a piece of paper. The man took it and folded it into his pocket. Then he reached over the counter and shook hands with Charlie. Lizzie turned and scuttled away. She didn't want to be seen again and Charlie himself might notice her and wonder why she was still hanging around. She went back to the factory and into Nellie's office.

'Have you got anything to eat?' she asked. 'Only I'm starving and I didn't bring anything with me.'

'I've got sandwiches you can share. Mrs Potts always makes far too much lunch for me. How was Charlie? Pleased to see you?'

'He was busy. Too busy to spend any time with me. But he was pleased the proofs were OK.'

'Is something wrong?'

'Well, not really. Charlie was a bit anxious to get rid of me and I saw someone go into the shop after I left. Someone I vaguely recognised, but I can't think from where. He looked through the proofs of our new brochure.'

'How do you know?'

'I watched from the other side of the road.'

'And you thought you knew him?'

'Not really. I've just seen him before. He looked at me, but didn't seem to recognise me.'

'I suppose you haven't seen him here?' Lizzie stared at her sister and gave a start.

'Yes, at that dinner thing you gave. When I pretended to be Jenny.'

'Where was he sitting?'

'Next to Mr Apperly's wife.'

'That was Abraham Brown. Brown's Pottery. They do earthenware dinner services. I wasn't sure why James invited him that evening, but then I don't always understand the way James's mind works. Especially not when we're entertaining.'

'No wonder he didn't recognise me. Nobody notices servants, do they?'

'I suppose you're right. Now, eat up if you're so hungry. I'll ask Clarrie to make some tea to go with it.'

Lizzie pondered over Charlie's odd behaviour, but finally dismissed it when she settled down to her typing again. Her ideas were coming together for the article and she began writing it later in the afternoon. Maybe she should consider James's offer of a job. It would mean she was earning wages and she could write in her spare time. When she arrived home that evening, her mother was anxiously waiting for her.

'There's a letter come from the Evening Post. The one you've been waiting for. Come on, I've been dying to open it all afternoon.'

With trembling fingers, Lizzie ripped

open the envelope and scanned the page.

'They don't want me,' she said at last. *Not sufficient skills for the position. Interested in my application and would urge me to gain shorthand qualifications and re-apply when it is up to speed.* They just haven't taken on board that I wanted a journalist position, not secretarial. Mind you, Mr what's-his-name said I'd need shorthand to be a reporter so maybe I'd better go to some evening classes and learn it. Ah well. Just as well I've got an alternative. Our James has offered me a job.'

'That's wonderful. At least you'd know that was safe.'

'Seems our entire family owes everything to James. We all work for him. He provides us with a home and everything.'

'Joe doesn't work for him. He's made his own way.'

'I suppose. I'm not sure what James has in mind, but I can still do my writing in my spare time.' She outlined her plan to her mother and they laughed over her plans for a pseudonym. 'Mind you, after my outburst about him not sending little William away, James might have changed his mind.'

'Oh Lizzie, you didn't? James wouldn't like you interfering.'

'Maybe not, but it had to be said. Look what a mess he is with relationships. He's quite cold actually. Still, I expect Nellie loves him. But it might say something about why they haven't had more children.'

'Lizzie stop it, right now. You are interfering in what goes on in someone's marriage and that is certainly not your place.'

'Maybe not, but it might explain something you've always gone on about.'

'Go and get ready for dinner. Ben will be home in a minute and he'll be hungry.'

The subject was closed for discussion, but not in Lizzie's mind. She really hoped her little nephew would be spared from all this formality and would continue to grow up with the people who loved him.

Besides, it would make sure Jenny kept her job and that would be better for Ben. Perhaps she had better stop thinking about all these other things and concentrate on helping Ben and Jenny to sort out their relationship.

It was high time there was another wedding in the family. She'd quite like to be a bridesmaid again.

An Accusation

For the next few weeks, Lizzie went to the factory each day and to evening classes two nights a week. She was making progress with the shorthand and her typing was improving rapidly.

James offer of a permanent job had never been formalised, but Nellie made sure she had a few pounds each week. She did a number of odd jobs, helping in various departments. When she arrived one morning, Nellie had some news for her.

'Clarrie has handed in her notice. Evidently, she is expecting a baby and her husband wants her to stay at home. She's not been very well lately. So, I wondered if you'd take on her work? It's partly as my assistant and some typing of course. Letters and a few invoices. What do you think? I know it isn't exactly what you were hoping for but at least it's a proper job and I'll enjoy working with you.'

'Thanks, Nellie. I'll take it, but as long as you know I'll still hope to be a reporter one day.'

'Of course you do. But at least you'll be able to write your articles and I won't mind if you do some work on it when I don't need you.'

'Thank you so much. You're a good sister to me.'

'I expect you to work for your wages so don't think I'm giving you an easy job. Clarrie wants to go at the end of this week so make sure you spend as much time as you can with her and learn everything you need to know from her.'

After the weeks of drifting around, it was good to have something positive to do. Lizzie was determined to prove herself and make sure everyone knew she was good at her job and not just swanning along in her sister's shade. She quickly learned the filing system and saw that improvements could be made. She said nothing to Clarrie. There would be plenty of time later, when she had gone and she was herself in charge.

There was more good news, which Lizzie felt might be partly down to her. James had decided that William should not be sent away to a boarding school, but would continue to attend a local day prep school and they would then consider boarding school when he was older.

Her relationship with Charlie was continuing and nothing had ever been said about the day she had called at the shop and received such short shrift. The brochures had been delivered in record time and several more smaller orders placed with him.

They went to the cinema regularly and finally, he had taken her to a dance. She had loved it and came away humming various tunes, much to her mother's annoyance. Lizzie felt her life was great and going almost exactly the way she had planned.

'I've finished my first article for the Post,' she told James. 'I've brought it for you to read before I send it in.'

'I'm busy right now, but if you leave it with me, I'll read it very soon,' he promised.

She went back to the room she now called her office and waited on tenterhooks. She had spent a great deal of her time working to make it perfect and was desperate for her brother-in-law's approval. It was almost the end of the day before James came into the office.

'This is a fine piece of work, Lizzie. You've got a good balance between fact and human interest. I'm sure the Post will take it and print it. Do you want me to have a word with the Editor?'

'No thank you, James. I want to succeed on my own merits and not on knowing a friend of his. I'm planning to use a pseudonym anyway, so he won't be prejudiced at all cos I'm a girl.'

'I see. Interesting. Well, I wish you luck with it. Very good.'

Glowing with pleasure at the praise, she set to work to type a covering letter. With a flourish, she hoped was sufficiently manly looking, she signed the name. *Giles Trentham*.

'And may you be taken on as a regular contributor,' she muttered as she licked the envelope. 'Now, should I post it or deliver it by hand?'

'What did you say?' Nellie asked as she came into the room.

'Talking to myself. Post it, I think.'

'Oh, your article. I gather James was impressed.'

'He certainly was. Fingers crossed for me.'

'Of course. You've worked hard on it and I hope they take it and pay you heaps of money.'

'You know something? I don't exactly care about the money as long as it gets printed.'

'Dear little Lizzie. I know what you mean. The first time I saw one of my designs in production, I would never have cared if I didn't get a penny. The pleasure of seeing my work produced and ready for the public to see, was quite enough compensation. Good luck anyway. Oh and yes, you should post it. Much more professional.'

She steeled herself for a long wait and decided to go shopping on the following Saturday. She needed to buy her new clothes and had saved a few pounds from her wages.

She went up to Hanley on the bus to look in the larger stores. There were two main stores which sold everything from screws and nails to high fashion clothing.

She walked through the first area and sniffed appreciatively at the perfumes and cosmetics counters. She had never used either, knowing how much her mother disapproved. She might treat herself to something, specially for Charlie one day but today, clothes were her main target.

She worked her way through the long racks and tried on a couple of things. But there was no way she would buy anything at the first stop. This clothes shopping thing was something new to her and she had to make the most of it. She wanted to get ideas and go the other shops before making her choices. Besides, she was after as much as she could find for her money.

By lunchtime, Lizzie was hungry and treated herself to a cup of tea and a bun in the cafeteria at one of the stores. She had almost decided on two outfits and was going back to the first store to look at them again to be sure they were just right. As she went in, she noticed the window display.

There was a complete selection of Nellie's latest design. The Debut Range it was called only this one was called something else. *Brownlow.*

Dinner and tea sets and a number of matching dishes. Only it didn't look quite right. There was something different about it. She looked more closely, but she couldn't be sure. Besides, as far as she knew, it hadn't actually been released yet.

The manufacturing process was only just getting underway. Frowning slightly, she went inside to the china department and went to the large display stand. She picked up one of the pieces and weighed it in her hand. It was heavy. Much heavier than usual Cobridge pieces. The delicate gold banding was replaced by a heavier, green line round the tops of the dishes and plates.

'Lovely, isn't it?' the assistant asked.

'Not bad. Who makes it?' She turned it over and looked for the manufacturer's stamp.

'You can buy all the pieces separately. A new idea. Instead of buying a set number for a dinner service, you can buy six, eight or what you will. Then the buyer can build up the set gradually. Useful for wedding presents too. People who can't afford a whole dinner service can buy a few pieces and that way the happy couple get the set of their dreams.'

Lizzie had heard those very words

only a few weeks ago, spoken by Nellie.

'And the maker is?'

'Brown's Pottery. Hence the name *Brownlow*. Very reasonable prices too.'

'It's earthenware. We only ever use fine bone china. Good day.'

Almost shaking with rage, Lizzie forgot all about her shopping and caught the bus home. She went straight to Nellie's and poured out her anger to her sister.

'It's exactly your design, but made in earthenware. Heavy as lead by comparison but it's your exact pattern and your idea of selling it all piece by piece instead of in complete sets.'

'I see. Well, other people do market in that way. Piece by piece, I mean. But it certainly looks as if someone has sold my ideas to a rival.'

'But you're always so careful about letting people see your work.' She stopped. Her heart suddenly raced as she thought of someone who had recently visited the factory and been shown Nellie's designs. He had also

185

been in contact with Mr Brown of Brown's Pottery.

Her face paled and she grabbed the side of the table, feeling as if she might faint.

'Lizzie, darling, what's the matter.'

'I've just realised we know someone who visited your design studio and who spoke to Mr Brown . . . '

'Oh, Lizzie. No. Not Charlie? Surely he wouldn't do anything like that?'

'I told you he saw Mr Brown too and wanted to get rid of me in a hurry that day when I took the proofs back. I saw him drawing something for Mr Brown as well. Oh, Nellie, what am I going to do? I really like Charlie. We have fun together, but if he's been spying and selling our designs, I can't possibly go on seeing him.'

'We mustn't jump to conclusions. It may not be him of course, although it does look pretty black for him. I need to think for a while. See how we can handle this.'

'I'm supposed to be seeing him

tonight. We're going to listen to music of some sort or another. I can't do it though, can I? I'll have to wait till he comes to pick me up and tell him I can't go.' Her voice was rising to a crescendo and when she stopped speaking, she burst into tears.

'You have to see him. After all, it might not have been him at all. See if he says anything during the evening. I must say though, he did seem particularly interested in everything we're doing. And he was very keen to see all our collection at home.'

'I can't bear it. The first man I meet who shows an interest in me and it turns out to be wretched Cobridge's China he's interested in after all.'

'Now stop it, Lizzie. Stop being so dramatic. You don't know it was him. Just forget it and go out and enjoy yourself this evening. We don't know it was him, remember. Keep calm and if you do ask questions, make them subtle ones. Don't come straight out with it.'

'I'll try, but it's so hard. He seemed so nice.'

'He still is nice. Don't forget that.'

'All right. If he is guilty though, I'll never forgive him. Oh dear, this is all so dreadful. But, I'd better go home now and change. With all of this going on, I never even bought a single thing. I was so looking forward to something new and stylish for my evening out.'

'Let's go and look in my wardrobe. There must be something there you could wear. Now what sort of music is it? Classical or something modern?'

'Modern, I think. Some dance band, but without the dancing.'

'Come on then. Let's see what I can find.'

Clutching two bags, Lizzie finally left Cobridge house quite late. She only had time to change and drink a cup of tea and eat a sandwich. Considering she'd had very little for lunch, she was feeling quite hungry. Perhaps Charlie would buy some fish and chips on the way home.

She ran upstairs to change without telling her mother about the disaster she had discovered. Industrial spying, it was and her Charlie could possibly be the guilty party.

'You look nice, love. Is that one of our Nellie's outfits? I thought you were buying new stuff.'

'I was, but didn't see anything I specially liked. Nellie's been having a turn out and I'm in luck. Where's Ben?'

'Gone to meet Jenny. He was acting sort of strange. I think he may be going to pop the question. Don't say anything though. He'll tell us in his own good time.'

'He's gone early enough. William's nowhere near his bedtime so Jenny will be busy for ages yet.'

'I think Nellie was looking after him this evening. James has gone to some do or other. I was thinking of going round to keep Nellie company instead of sitting here on my own.'

'Good idea. I did think we might come back for a cup of something after the concert. We might get chips as I haven't had a proper meal today. Shall we bring some for you?'

'No ta. If I do go to Nellie's I'll have something there.' There was a knock at the door. 'That'll be your fellow. Do you want to bring him in?'

'No thanks, Mum. We'd best get off or we'll miss the start. Will you be all right walking round to Nellie's on your own?'

'Course I will. Get off with you and have a nice time.'

Lizzie took a deep breath and fixed a smile on her face as she opened the door.

'Hello, Charlie. I'm all ready to go.'

'Good. Let's get on our way.' He took her hand and tucked it into his own arm. He smiled down at her and asked how she was.

Be normal. Act as if nothing happened. It might not have done.

'I'm worn out with shopping. Didn't find anything I wanted to find. Not at all.'

'But isn't this a new outfit? I haven't seen it before. It's lovely. Suits you.'

'Thanks. Truth be told, it's one of our Nellie's. She didn't want it any more and gave it to me. Knowing her, I bet it cost the earth. Far more than I could ever afford anyway. It's so good we're the same size. Lucky for me. I'm a bit taller but then, shorter skirts are quite fashionable, aren't they?'

'I don't know much about fashion.' They walked along in silence for a few minutes.

After jabbering away at the beginning she suddenly felt there was nothing to say. He'd probably think that was odd as she always talked nineteen-to-the-dozen.

'Did you ever hear anything about that article you wrote?' he asked.

'No. But I think that's sort of normal. If it wasn't commissioned, they leave it on the heap till someone's got time to read it.'

'Must be frustrating for you.'

'A bit, but there's plenty for me to do.'

'You seem to be enjoying your work, despite the reservations.'

'I am actually.'

'Right, it's just round this corner. I hope you're going to like this music. I didn't say before, but it's a sort of club room. I'm not sure your mother would approve. There's a pie and chips supper in the interval and they serve plenty of soft drinks as well beer and things.'

'I'm glad about the pie and chips. I haven't ever got round to a proper meal today.'

Charlie handed two tickets to the man on the door and they went inside. There were small tables set round the room, with four seats at most of them.

'Where do you want to sit?'

'Near enough to see, but not so near we're deafened.'

They selected a table in the middle and sat down.

'I'll go and get drinks. Lemonade or something different?'

'I'll go mad and have orange juice this time. Thanks.' He left and she watched him. He was so good looking and he seemed quite keen on her. She didn't want to believe he was only seeing her because she had connections with Cobridge's.

But the clues were there and everything pointed to him as the betrayer. Or spy, as she was thinking, as it sounded more dramatic. She had to find a way to broach the subject. The place was filling up and noise levels rising. Charlie returned and sat down.

'Can I ask you something?' she began. This was it. She got no further as someone came and stopped at their table.

'Charlie? Charlie Swift? Couldn't believe it was you in a place like this. How are you?'

'Davey. Good to see you. Lizzie, this is an old school friend of mine. Davey, meet Lizzie.'

'I say, do you mind if we join you? Only there aren't any more tables left. My wife is just pushing her way through the crowds. Busy, isn't it?'

That was the end of any chance of conversation. Maybe it was just as well, Lizzie decided. This was hardly the place to discuss anything so important.

It was a pleasant enough evening. The band were good though probably better placed in a dance hall. The toe tapping was a bit restricted by the lack of space. Davey and his wife, May, were very nice but even when the supper was served, it was too noisy to say much. As they were leaving, Davey almost shouted to them, 'We should meet up again. Perhaps you'd like to come and have a meal with us sometime?'

'Thanks. That would be great. You'd like that wouldn't you, love?' he asked Lizzie. 'They've got a lovely little baby. How old is she now?'

'Almost six months. Granny's doing the baby-sitting duties this evening. But, we should get back. I'll give you a call soon. Same number, is it?'

'Yes indeed. Been great to see you again.'

Lizzie felt slightly left out. They all

knew each other well and she was a new person in the group. But it might be all right. At least she now had things to ask on the way home. She didn't want to spoil things by asking questions about spying after such a nice evening.

Instead she asked about his school friend and his wife. When they reached her home, there were no lights on. Her mother must still be at Nellie's. She didn't want to ask Charlie in when she was alone. She would have relished it even just a few days ago, but now everything was different.

'I'll see you soon. Thanks for a lovely evening.'

'Aren't you going to invite me in for a cup of tea or something?'

'I'm sorry, but I feel exhausted. Next time maybe.'

'Is everything all right?' he asked. 'Only you seem a bit out of sorts. You have been all evening.'

'I'm just tired.'

'All right. As you like. Don't I get a goodnight kiss?'

'Course.' She put her arms round his neck and pulled him down towards her. His lips were gentle and she nearly weakened and invited him into the house, but she knew that was much too dangerous.

She might be losing him any time now and didn't want to make it any harder than it seemed at this moment. 'Good night, Charlie,' she whispered. 'I had a good time. Thanks.'

'Good night. Lizzie, everything's all right, isn't it? Between us I mean. You haven't met someone else, have you?'

'Course not. Like I said, I am really tired. I've had a busy week and with shopping all day . . . '

'All right. Only I don't want you keeping things from me. I want you to feel able to trust me. You know you can tell me anything you like.'

'Oh, Charlie . . . I have to go. Goodnight.' She pulled out her key and went inside before she could blurt out something she might regret.

Once she had shut the door, she

leaned on it, thinking she had probably missed the perfect opportunity to ask him for the truth. But, as Nellie had said, it would be wrong to make any sort of accusations without proof.

Everything so far was circumstantial, damning though it seemed. But she could think of nobody else who could be guilty. With a sigh, she went to put the kettle on. Cups of tea were the cure all for everything, or so her mother thought. She sat in front of what was left of the fire, clutching a mug of tea, trying to decide what to do next.

'Lizzie? You at home?' called her mother as she came in. 'Thanks for the lift, Nellie. Night, night.'

'Hello, Mum. Had a nice evening?'

'Lovely, ta. William was really funny and we had a nice meal together, just the three of us. He's really growing up now. I was a bit worried about our Nellie though. She seemed a bit stressed about something, but she wouldn't say what. How was your evening?'

'It was good, thanks. We met a school friend of Charlie's and his wife. They've asked us for a meal sometime.'

'That's nice. It's good you're meeting people outside the factory. Broaden your interests. Are you seeing Charlie tomorrow?'

'No. Now I'm working properly, I need some time to myself.'

'I see. Everything's all right though, isn't it? You've not had a row or anything?'

'Not really. Just got something on my mind.'

'You and Nellie are a right pair. Always were. Well, I'm off to bed now. I've got to be up for early chapel tomorrow. Why don't you come with me? Whatever's bothering you, it might help to ask someone of a greater power for help?'

'I don't think so, thanks. I need to think a bit for myself. Ben hasn't come back yet. He's late, isn't he?'

'I left him chatting in the kitchen at Nellie's. That Mrs Potts thinks the sun shines out of him so she's let him stay on late. I wasn't told if there's any news yet. You know, regarding Jenny.'

'Maybe she said no.'

'I doubt that. The way they were all laughing in there. Chances are, he just hasn't got round to it yet.'

'All in good time. Well, I'm off to bed myself now.'

It seemed Nellie had said nothing about the problems to Nan so Lizzie was not about to launch into her own concerns so late at night. Instead, she was to lie awake for many hours, trying to come to terms with the situation.

She racked her brains to think of anyone else who had the sort of knowledge that had been passed on. The girls in Nellie's department were all completely trustworthy, as far as they knew. Vera, the manager, always kept a very tight rein on all of them. There had been one or two bad eggs in the past, but they were all long gone.

All her thinking yielded nothing and she was still left with the problem of

Charlie. However she tackled it in the long run, they had made no plans for seeing each other again so everything was on hold. She finally fell asleep near dawn.

'I've brought you some tea, Lizzie. I'm just off to chapel. Put the oven on if I'm not back by ten-thirty will you?'

'Mum? What time is it?'

'Nearly nine o'clock. Make sure you don't go back to sleep. Ben's gone to get a newspaper, but he'll be back in a minute. Are you feeling all right?'

'Didn't sleep much, but I'm OK. I'm awake now so don't worry.'

She pottered around all morning, feeling restless and wondering what to say when she went to Nellie's that afternoon. Perhaps they could find a moment to be on their own to discuss matters.

They were finishing the washing up after lunch when there was a knock at the door. Nan went to answer it.

'It's your Charlie. Come to see if you wanted to go for a walk.'

'Oh, dear,' Lizzie muttered. But she wiped her hands and took off her apron.

'He's in the sitting room. You go, love, and I'll finish off in the kitchen. You weren't expecting him, I gather?'

'No. I said I wasn't. I'm in all my old clothes, but he'll have to put up with that.'

She went through to the sitting room where Ben had been reading the sports news. The two were chatting like old friends.

'Hello. I wasn't expecting to see you today,' she said to Charlie.

'I was a bit worried about you. You seemed so out of sorts last night and I wanted to make sure you were all right.'

'I'm fine, thanks.'

'So, how about a walk?'

'I suppose so.'

'Not if you don't want to, of course. But I'll stand you tea at the pavilion if you'd like to.'

She hesitated, but decided that she needed to face up to the problems.

Walking in the park would give them a chance to talk and that was what she needed most.

'I'd better just go and change. I'm too scruffy to be seen out on a Sunday.'

'You might as well sit down, Charlie. Her changing takes at least an hour to choose what to wear and half an hour to change. Then she'll decide something else would have been better any road.'

'I'll give you a hiding one of these days, our Ben. You can both time me. I'll be back in five minutes. Or maybe ten.' She ran up the stairs, determined to prove her brother was all wrong about her.

With Nellie's latest offerings, she made her choice immediately and was down again in seven minutes. 'See, he doesn't know anything about me at all,' she announced triumphantly. 'Come on then. Let's leave this lazy bones to read his paper.'

'You seem a bit more cheerful this afternoon.'

'Well, I've decided I need to talk to you about some things and now I've made up my mind to do it.' They were reaching the park and went in through the large wrought iron gates.

'That sounds ominous. Have I done something wrong?'

'Well, that's what I'm not sure about. You might have done and I need to know.'

Charlie looked puzzled.

'You'd better ask. Shall we sit over there? There's nobody else near that seat.'

'The flower beds are all done now. I suppose there's not much to look at here, now. Besides, it's got a bit chilly for sitting around.'

'Does that mean you don't want to sit here?' Lizzie frowned. She knew she was prevaricating and trying to find excuses to put off the problem.

'No, it's OK. It'll be too crowded in the pavilion. This is all very difficult for me, but here goes.'

Charlie looked grim.

'Are you about to tell me you don't want to see me any more? Because if so, just get on with it. I can't bear this much longer. If it's because I haven't done something you wanted, then you could ask me. If it's because we've been seeing each other for a while and I haven't asked you to marry me, then it's because I was being cautious. You're very young and I wanted to give you chance to grow a little more. That's not a criticism, it's just fact. Besides, I'm in no position to have a wife to look after.'

'Shut up, Charlie. It's nothing like that. I don't want to be engaged to you or anyone else. Not yet awhile anyhow. No, it's something really serious. Someone, a rival manufacturer, has copied all of Nellie's latest designs. The whole concept and idea behind it all.

'Nobody goes into her private office so very few people have actually seen it. And the manufacturer is Brown's Pottery and I saw Mr Brown in your office the day I came round with the proofs. You wanted to get rid of me as fast as you could. I saw you drawing something for him as well.'

'Are you saying you think I passed on Nellie's designs to him?' He went pale and looked as if he was about to be sick, or that was Lizzie's interpretation of his reaction.

'It looks suspicious, you must admit.'

'How could you possibly think I'd do something like that?' he spluttered. He stood up and walked away from her. He clenched his hands behind his back and stared at the empty flower beds in front of him. He swung round and with tight lips and a furious expression, said, 'I think I'd better walk you home.'

'Don't bother. I'll see myself home.' She got up and walked briskly to the gates.

She decided immediately that she would go to Nellie's, where the family usually gathered on a Sunday. She turned the opposite way to her home and walked off.

She glanced back once, but there was no sign of Charlie following her. He had not denied it. His anger when she spoke was probably understandable, but all he had said was, *How could you possibly think I'd do something like that?* It was hardly a denial, was it? She rang the bell and Ethel came to let her in.

'They're all in the drawing room. Seems we get to see the whole mob of you today.'

'I thought that was Joe's father-in-law's car. Joe and Daisy are here too, are they?'

'Came to break the good news. She's expecting. 'Bout time. They've been married long enough.'

'That's nice. I'll go and congratulate them.'

'Don't say as I told you. They'll accuse me of listening behind doors.'

'And how did you find out?'

'Listening behind the door of course,' she giggled.

'You're terrible, Ethel.'

'Isn't your fellow with you today? Right handsome, he is. I'd always have

206

him if you don't want him.'

'Bit young for you, isn't he?'

'I'm not fussy. He'd do me fine.'

'No chance there, I'm afraid. I'll pretend to be surprised when they tell me the news, don't worry.'

'Thanks, Lizzie.' She pushed the drawing room door open and went in to join her family.

'Hello, everyone. Cut short my walk as it looked like rain.'

'Really? I thought it looked quite nice,' Joe said. 'How are you, little sister?'

'I'm OK, thanks. And you?'

'We're both very well indeed, aren't we, love?'

'We've got some news,' Daisy said shyly. 'I'm expecting.'

'Oh, that's lovely. Great news. Congratulations. Both of you. All three of you.'

The family were all wreathed in smiles. Nan was bursting with joy.

'Another grandchild, it's wonderful. Quite made my day. I was praying for them at chapel this morning. Almost as if I knew there was some exciting news coming.'

The excited chatter went on and gave Lizzie the chance to reflect on her own feelings.

Nellie glanced at her a few times and guessed she had spoken to Charlie of their suspicions. She would have to get her on one side as soon as she could and question her about Charlie's reaction.

'What happened to that young man of yours? Thought he was taking you out for tea?' Ben asked.

'Change of plan. That's all. Now tell me, when's this babby of yours due?'

'Should be here in April. Near enough anyway.'

'Lovely. A spring baby with all the nicer weather to come. Good start for him or her.'

'My busy time with all the farm work. Calving. Planting crops and everything. Cutting silage.'

'I bet your mum and dad are pleased,

aren't they?' she asked Daisy.

'I think so. Except my dad's worried about who's going to manage all the dairy work and such.'

The conversation droned on with Lizzie trying hard to take an interest, but her own heart felt as if it was slowly breaking into a hundred pieces. It was the end of her first romance. The look on Charlie's face suggested that he would never want to see her again, whether he was guilty or not.

The accusation was too much for him to bear. She had handled the whole thing badly, accusing him as she had done. What did everyone say? Plenty more fish in the sea. But everyone also said, there's no love like your first love. Charlie had been her first love and she had lost him.

A Search For The Truth

'I found a couple more things you might like,' Nellie whispered later. 'Do you want to come and look?'

'Thanks. That's very good of you.' She followed Nellie up the stairs to the big bedroom.

'Sorry, but that was just an excuse to talk to you in private. You look so upset, I gather you spoke to Charlie? What did he say?'

'All he said was, 'How could you possibly think I'd do something like that?' Then he turned away from me and went very pale. He hardly said another word except that he would walk me home. I told him not to bother. Then I came here. Oh Nellie, I'm so miserable. Just to think he might have done something so terrible and so mean.'

'I'm sorry, love. Come here.' She

hugged her sister close to her and then wiped away the tears that had formed in Lizzie's eyes. 'You'll meet lots of other men. You're still young.'

'I know. That's what Charlie said. But he was my first boyfriend. I loved being with him.'

'I know. I know. Now, I'd better find something for you to wear, to make sure nobody guesses we were just talking. I'll discuss it all with James this evening. I didn't have the opportunity last night as he was out.'

'You gave me lots of new things yesterday, so don't worry. We can say it didn't fit or something.'

'There are a couple of hats that may be of use. Take those.'

'You're good to me, Nellie. Always were. So what about Daisy and Joe's news?' She sniffed hard as she tried to change the subject.

'It's lovely for them. I know Daisy's been wanting to start a family for ages. For years in fact, since they were first married. But you know Joe. Has to have things certain before he'll take any risks.'

'Didn't you ever want more children?'

'Course I did. But it never happened. But we have our William and he's such a joy.'

'I love William, but I'm not sure I ever want to have children. This world's a funny place to bring up a kiddy.'

'You will, when you meet the right man. But you're still ambitious. Still young enough to do something with life. No news about the article yet?'

'Not yet. But I'm not that worried. Besides, I've got a good job now with plenty to keep me occupied. It's a pity I can't make an excuse to visit Brown's Pottery to say I'm writing an article about them. I could do some spying of my own.'

'That's not such a bad idea, but probably a bit risky. He might recognise you. You and I are quite alike and he knows me quite well.'

'Yes, but does he know your maiden

name? There's no reason he should. I quite like this idea.'

'Now Lizzie, you mustn't do anything stupid. Let me talk it all through with James this evening and we'll discuss it tomorrow. Now, we'd better get back to the others or they'll think we've left the party for good. Tea-time now, I think. Go and wash your face. There are still a few tear stains left.'

Lizzie seemed to be in something of a dream for the rest of the day. She kept re-living her conversation with Charlie and wondering how she could have handled it better. It hurt so much. What was she going to do on Saturday evenings? Would she ever be able to face walking in the park again?

She kept speculating about what James might have said and if he blamed her for introducing Charlie to the company. If it hadn't been for her insisting on getting the new brochure printed, he would never have visited the factory.

By Monday morning, she had decided

she was totally responsible for the whole catastrophe and that James would never want to speak to her again. She sat at the typewriter and began to type the pile of letters that Nellie must have left for her. She kept looking round to see if Nellie had come in yet, but she was presumably having a meeting with James and possibly, some of the sales team.

She desperately needed to know what they were saying and tried to think of an excuse to go to the board room. If they all blamed her, then she might as well leave right away. It was almost lunchtime before Nellie came to the office.

'What's the news?' she asked.

'Not good, I'm afraid. We were getting orders for the new line but they've stopped dead, now there's a cheaper version of the same thing. Trouble is, we've made considerable investment setting up the production line for this and now we're strapped for cash flow.'

'Can't you still use the shapes and

put a different pattern, design on them?'

'It all takes time. You can't just use the same pattern on each item. You have to scale it down and make it fit each shape while retaining the lines.'

'I think I understand. What about the lithographing thing you use? Isn't there something you could use with that? Save time hand painting, doesn't it?'

'Well, yes. Maybe we could use some of the standard outline shapes and hand paint the design inside. Hmm. I'll go and have a think. You may have had an idea there. We'll make a designer of you yet.'

That was all she saw of Nellie for the rest of the day. She took a cup of tea in during the afternoon and removed the cold cupful she had left earlier. At the end of the day, she left the pile of letters for Nellie to check and sign and went home. She still had no idea of James's true reaction to the suspected spying episode.

Her day improved enormously when

she got home and found a letter from the Evening Post.

'Mum, guess what? They want to publish my article in a weekly special about the Potteries. *'Will you please arrange to call at the office to discuss terms and possible future projects.'* How about that? Not only do they like his one, they might want me to do more.'

'So who is Giles Trentham? I nearly gave it back to the postman thinking he'd left it by mistake.'

'It's my pen name. They don't like women writers so I decided I'd be a man.'

'So what are you going to do about this call at the office bit? Are you going to wear a false moustache or something?'

'Oh. I never thought of that. Perhaps we can communicate by letter. I can say I'm a recluse and never go out.'

'So how do you manage to do the interviews with everyone?'

'Ah. Problems all the way. I could

write a letter to them first time and when they decide how much they'll pay me and I've got the money safely, I can reveal the truth. Da-da.' She made a sweeping gesture and knocked over a chair.

'You sure you wouldn't rather be an actress?' Nan said. 'Only you seem to be making a big drama out of everything. Besides, they'll want to pay you by cheque and this Giles whatsit doesn't have a bank account. Nor do you, come to that. How much do you think they'll offer?'

'Don't ask me. What do I know about anything? I'm just the creative inspiration behind good old Giles.'

'You never do anything that's straightforward do you, our Lizzie?' She gave a little chuckle. 'Ah well, I'd better get on with tea. I've got some chops. I hope Ben's not much longer coming. He's been working late the last few days.'

Lizzie took her precious letter up to her room and began to write a draft of her reply. She would type it tomorrow when she found a moment.

For a while, she quite forget the rest of the dramas in her life at present and glowed in the praise and joy of being accepted. *Very well presented and an interesting insight into the pottery industry.* Now she really did have an excuse to visit Brown's Pottery and ask a few questions there. She could call herself Gill Trentham and claim yet another pseudonym.

That way he could never associate her with Cobridge's. She would have to go there one day when Nellie could spare her, but that wouldn't be a problem, especially if she was going on her own spying mission for the company.

'You seem a bit more cheerful. Got over your row with Charlie, have you?'

'Not really. But I'm really pleased about my article. My name in print at last.'

'Only it's not really your name, is it? How was Nellie today? I thought she looked very tired yesterday. She does work too hard.'

'Haven't seen much of her. I think they're having to do some extra stuff. They were in a meeting all morning. Crikey, I forgot. It's my shorthand class tonight. I'd better change before we eat or I'll be late. Think I can hear Ben coming in.'

'Oh good. I'll set those chops under the grill.'

It was good to have something else to think about that evening. At the end of the session, she walked out with a couple of the other girls.

Now she considered herself to be almost a journalist, Lizzie felt she could ask questions about where they worked. It was all good insider information and as most people around here worked at one of the potbanks, it might all hold her in good stead when she wanted to do more interviews.

There was one young man in the group who always seemed rather shy. Once he'd got over being teased about becoming a secretary, he relaxed. He had spoken to Lizzie a few times and this evening, he attached himself to the others.

'We were just thinking of going for a coffee somewhere. Do you want to come?' one of the girls asked.

'Thanks,' said the young man at the same time as Lizzie said 'why not?' He sat next to her in the café.

'I'm Gregory,' he said holding out a hand. 'I'm just starting work at the Evening Post. They said I've got to learn shorthand, so here I am.'

'I'm Lizzie. I had an interview there, but as I'm a girl, they'd only want me as a secretary.'

'I'm only going to be very much a junior. Garden parties and jumble sales, I gather.'

'Still, you have to start somewhere. I'd be grateful for any of it.'

'Would you like ... I mean if you aren't already walking out with someone, would you like to come to the pictures or something with me?'

'I'm not sure. No offence, but I've only just broken up with my young man. I'm not really ready for a new relationship yet. But thanks for asking me.'

'Well, if you change your mind, let me know. I'll see you later in the week.'

'All right. Thanks, Gregory.'

'Shall I see you home?'

'It's all right. I don't have far to go.'

'But I'd like to. It's not safe for a pretty girl to be out alone after dark.'

She finally agreed and not knowing anything about him or where he lived, they walked together along the dark roads.

'I hope this isn't out of your way.'

'I live over the other side of town, but it isn't a problem. I like you, Lizzie. Noticed you the very first week. I didn't dare speak to you though cos you always looked so confident. So, you want to write do you?' She nodded.

She wondered if she should tell him about her article, but he might let something slip at the paper and that wouldn't help her plans at all.

'I am definitely going to be a writer.

221

I'd like it to be with newspapers, but I might even write a book for kiddies. My sister is a brilliant artist. She used to draw pictures for me when I was little and tell me stories. A lot of the pictures have been made into china plates now.'

'Wow. That sounds really impressive. If the books are successful, they'll sell more plates.'

'I never thought of that. What a good idea. I'll have to suggest it to my sister. When she isn't so busy.'

The conversation turned to wider issues and even touched on world affairs.

'Do you think there'll be another war?' she asked.

'I dunno. Some people think so, but others say they're negotiating. There's supposed to be some big speech coming in the next few days.'

'I only know what they said about the last war. It was supposed to be the war to end all wars, but then not everyone was happy about the way it ended. My dad was a miner so he was in what they called a reserved occupation. He didn't have to go away and fight.'

They reached the end of her street. For some reason she felt cautious about letting him know exactly where she lived. 'This is where I live. Thanks for seeing me home.'

'That's all right. I've enjoyed talking to you. It's nice to meet a girl who's interested in more than just clothes and a hair do. Goodnight, Lizzie.' To her surprise, he leaned over and kissed her cheek.

'Er . . . goodnight, Gregory.' She rushed away and went into the house still feeling slightly shocked. He was nice enough, but she certainly didn't want to be involved with anyone else just yet.

Out in the road, a shocked Charlie had been watching and waiting for her to return. He turned and walked quickly back to his home. He knew Lizzie attended her evening classes on a Monday and had been waiting to speak to her.

He had behaved badly after her accusation and had decided that he needed to provide her with an explanation. But she had come back home with a new man friend who had even kissed her. It must be someone from her evening class and he wondered how long this had been going on. He was angry and walked faster than ever to relieve his temper.

If he had spoken to her, goodness knows what he would have accused her of doing. If she had wanted to end their relationship, why didn't she just say instead of making those dreadful, hurtful accusations? He cursed his stupidity in the business too. He had produced all those brochures at a minimal profit, partly because of Lizzie and partly as a pitch for more business. Now he'd lost both of them.

Nan was listening to the radio when she went into the sitting room. She grinned when Lizzie arrived.

'There's been really good news. Mr Chamberlain has made a speech. 'Sleep in your beds' he said, 'I believe it is peace for our time.' All the worries about another dreadful war are over. That means everything can get going again. I know Nellie and James have been worried about the drop in sales and all that's to do with this threat of another war.'

'Oh, that really is good news. Funny, I was talking to one of the other students in the class about it just now. He'll be very pleased.'

'He? I thought it was a shorthand class?'

'He's been told he's got to learn it. He's got a job on the Post as a reporter. Lucky blighter. I told you they only want men reporters there. I'm just as good as he is, I know it. I didn't get the job because I can't do shorthand and now he gets it and he still can't do shorthand. It's not right. Not these days. Still, I've sold an article and all he'll be doing is reports of scout jumble sales and Sunday school outings.'

'Don't knock them. You were happy

enough to go on the Sunday School outings when you were little.'

'I'm not knocking it. I did enjoy them, of course I did.' She yawned. 'I'm off to bed now. I'm really tired. It's good news though, about the war. Night.'

She lay awake for awhile, but felt happier than she had done last night. There were still problems ahead, but two lots of good news on one day had made all the difference. Cobridge's were still in difficulties and that had to be resolved. Not really her problem, but she still felt very involved.

* * *

Everyone was talking about Mr Chamberlain's speech and a more positive future and the news had spread round the whole factory. There was excited chatter all around.

Nellie was in the office early next day. She looked tired and Lizzie was concerned.

'Are you all right?' she asked. 'You look very pale.'

'Just tired. I worked late last night. Trying to come up with something new in a hurry. Something that doesn't cost too much to produce, but still has the Cobridge stamp on it.'

'Someone suggested that if we ever got round to writing those books for children, you could make china to go with the stories. The fairy plates are there already, but it could improve sales.'

'Good idea for sometime in the future. I've got too much going on already for the time being.'

'Oh, and best of all, the Post has accepted my article. They want me to call in at the office to discuss payments and maybe discuss more articles. So I can legitimately visit Brown's with a perfect excuse.'

'Lizzie, well done. That's terrific news. But didn't you use another name?'

'That's the problem. If I go in, my

cover's blown. If I don't, they'll send a cheque made out to someone who doesn't exist.'

'If they like the article, they'll buy it anyway. I can always cash a cheque for you, so don't worry. You have to sign on the back and I can pay it into our account.'

'I've decided to write to them anyway and accept and ask what they're offering. Anyway, what did James have to say about the spying thing?'

'He doesn't really think it could have been Charlie. Unless he has talents we don't know about, he would never have had enough time to make enough notes or anything.'

'Really? That's terrific. I thought he was going to blame me for bringing him into the factory. But I did accuse him. Oh heavens, how can I make it up to him?'

She knew what she had said to Charlie must have hurt his feelings dreadfully. 'He must have been really upset at my accusation. I don't know how I can ever put things right. So, who does James think is the guilty party?'

'It might have been Brown himself. Look, this is very confidential. You mustn't tell anyone.'

'Course not. What's the big mystery?'

'You know business hasn't been good lately?' Lizzie nodded. 'Well, James has been looking for a partner. Another company we can merge with. That way, we can bring in new methods, tunnel kilns and such like. Too expensive for one company to buy, but sharing the costs might make economic sense.'

'So you think Mr Brown has been to look round here and stole the designs himself?'

'It looks that way. But he definitely needed help from the inside. I have to speak to Vera and see who's new in the decorating shop. Difficult, but we need to know. I've arranged to see her later this morning. Actually, you can sit in on the interview. Use your newfound skills at shorthand to make notes. But you must remain quiet and not interfere.'

'As if I would,' Lizzie burst out.

'Yes, well that *as if* had better be right. She's coming in at ten, once she's got the girls going for the day.'

Lizzie's shorthand skills needed a lot more practise, but she managed to catch the gist of the discussion between Nellie and Vera. There were three fairly new girls who had been employed in the past three months.

'You did check their references, I hope?' Nellie asked.

'Of course. But it's easy enough to forge them and give a telephone number that connects to someone they know. They can then give the answers we need to hear. I suppose you know about the Brown Pottery copying our stuff, do you?'

'When did you find out about it?'

'Saturday. I was shopping and saw it in one of the stores. I would have told you yesterday, but you seemed to be in meetings all day. I guessed you knew. So this is why you're asking about the new girls?'

'Is there a likely candidate among them, do you think?'

'I wouldn't like to point a finger.'

They discussed a number of the girls and who had particular skills at painting different things. The designs in question involved a lot of different techniques so a number of people had been working on them.

The gilders who painted the gold rims, possibly most expensive of the raw constituents, had worked for Cobridge's for many years and were discounted from suspicion. The more intricate parts of the patterns were also painted by long standing members of the department.

'So, it really looks as if suspicion falls on one or more of the new girls. Keep a close eye on them and see if they do anything suspicious. I'll go and talk to George at the gatehouse and ask him if he's noticed anyone acting strangely. Trying to take stuff out. He's usually very conscientious, but he might not have realised if there had been sensitive material. OK. Thanks Vera. No other problems?'

'Well, not as such, but we are getting to the end of the orders. Are we intending to carry on with the Debut line?'

'I think we've gone too far with it to abandon it. The new shapes of dishes and so on, have cost a lot to alter the machines, so I'm working on alterations to the decoration. A plain band of colour inside the plate rim and a light floral border. The lids of the tureens will be plain in colour to match the banding. I also thought some of the extra sundry dishes could be plain colours to save so much work. This way, we might even reduce costs.'

'Sounds good. Well, let me know when you want us to start.'

'I'll get some patterns to you in a couple of days.'

Vera left and Lizzie smiled at her sister.

'Do you want me to type up my notes?'

'I think not. It was a good exercise for you, though. I'll have to watch what's going on there a little more. I've been too busy to look lately. Now, I'll go down to see George. If you want to type your letter to the Post, I'm happy for you to do that now.'

'Thanks, Nellie. I was going to do it during my dinner break.'

Nellie went to the gatehouse and asked George about his daily bag searches. It was the custom for him to look each day, especially on the way out, to make sure nobody was taking anything they shouldn't. She well remembered her own time as a junior worker when he looked into her little bag when she carried her dinner in and looked when it was empty when she was going home.

'Can't say I've seen anything odd. There's one or two started bringing a newspaper in to read at dinner, but I always thought that was innocent enough. Is there a problem, Mrs Nellie?'

'I'm afraid so. Our new designs have been copied. Every detail the same, but made in earthenware.'

'Eh, that's terrible. Which maker?'

'Brown's Pottery.'

'I've seen him sniffing round a few times lately. But as he was the boss's guest, I never looked in his briefcase. I never do when it's anyone like that. Was it him then?'

'He wouldn't have had the chance to copy things in so much detail. Someone must have drawn out detailed copies of the designs. Let me know who's been bringing in newspapers. They could have hidden drawings between the pages and you'd never have seen them.'

'Right. I'll make a list of anyone I can remember and I'll take a look between the pages in future. Oh, I can't tell you how sorry I am. And I'm ashamed of myself for not spotting it.'

'Don't worry, George. It's not your fault. It's someone who has been very cleverly cheating on us.'

It was later that day that George sent

up a list of everyone he could remember bringing in a newspaper. There were several of the paintresses, but mostly it was the men who worked at the clay end.

Workers from a few of the other departments were on the list, but it seemed the greater suspicion lay with the girls in the decorating department. Nellie studied the names and tried to picture their faces. Doubtless the men were bringing papers in to discuss sports news.

A lot of them couldn't read and relied on their mates to keep them up to date with the goings on in the football comments. She had often seen them arguing about the merits of either Port Vale or Stoke City when she went through the departments.

The girls were something new, though. They might have been interested in the news about the war, but even that was unlikely. She decided to walk through the decorating shop at lunch time and see what was going on with this new interest in the news.

It seemed innocent enough. She overheard a lot of laughter as they read out each other's star signs, a new addition to one of the more popular daily papers. Ribald comments flowed and giggles stemmed as she passed through the department.

She went for a word with Vera and asked her to watch out for anyone putting extra sheets of drawing paper inside the news. It was a bit like shutting the stable door after the horse had bolted, but was a safe guard for the future.

'Have any of the printed sheets of the designs gone missing?' she asked. Each bench had a sheet of the designs so they could be copied by the paintresses as they worked on the actual china.

'I suppose the usual few have gone when they got stuff spilled on them or torn. I'll check.'

'I think we shall have to start collecting them in at the end of each day. I know it's extra work, but it seems it may be necessary.'

When Nellie returned to her office, she found Lizzie sitting staring into space. She looked rather upset.

'What's wrong, love?'

'I've been thinking about Charlie. He must have been so agitated when I as good as accused him of spying. And now it seems it wasn't him in the first place. I might have ruined what was going to be my own future.'

'Perhaps you could write him a letter. Apologise to him and say you were upset and had made a terrible mistake.'

'But suppose he doesn't want to see me again?'

'Perhaps he won't, but at least you will have set the record straight. You'll have given him a chance to see you again if he wants to.'

'I'm not sure I'd forgive me if it was the other way round. Still, maybe you're right. I should write to him. Or should I go to the print shop to talk to him face to face?'

'Up to you. If it was me, I'd write.

Less upsetting for you if he's still so angry.'

'You're right. I'll do it tonight and post it on my way to work. I need to try and sort it out so that we can still do business with his company.'

'Good girl. You're becoming a loyal employee of Cobridge's. Putting our needs first.'

It was one of the most difficult things Lizzie had ever had to face and skilled though she was at writing, it involved more than mere words. Somehow, she had to express her sorrow at her mistake and at the same, let him know how much he meant to her.

She almost wondered if she should mention the word *l-o-v-e*, but decided against it as she wasn't entirely sure what it meant. As she sat in her room pondering over the difficult letter, she tried to decide. Who were the people she loved? She certainly loved her Mum, Nellie and Ben and Joe to some extent, thought she felt distanced from her older brother once he had moved to live away from home.

She loved little William, but had to admit she felt slightly scared of James. Nellie's husband was in a different class and was also the factory owner, a daunting figure in her life so that explained that. So how did Charlie fit into the love thing? She liked being with him. Liked it when they kissed.

She enjoyed his arm round her sometimes, when they walked. She thought about him such a lot when they were apart and always felt excited when she knew they were going to meet. But did all that mean love? How did she feel if she was never to see him again?

She contemplated the thought. Simple answer. She would be very upset. She even felt tears forming at the very thought.

'I think I must love him. Or I certainly will in a year or two.'

She finished her letter and put it in an envelope and sealed it so she couldn't do any more about it.

'I'm Glad We Cleared The Air'

'Did you write your letter, love?' asked Nan the next morning when Lizzie appeared downstairs.

'I did and I'll post it on my way to work.' Despite sealing the envelope last night, Lizzie had opened it again several times and finally had to find another envelope.

She had brought a few from work one day when she had asked Nellie if she could take one for her article. Her sister had given her a bundle of envelopes. She still felt uncertain about her words but felt that writing was the right thing to do.

Once she had posted it, she spent the next couple of days wondering what Charlie's reaction would be. She heard nothing. At least it was her evening class tonight so she wouldn't be sitting at home worrying.

Gregory was waiting for her at the door when she arrived at the community hall where the classes were held.

'Hello, Lizzie. I hoped you'd be here. Did you think any more about coming out with me?'

'I'm sorry, Gregory. I thought I'd made it clear that I don't want to go out with anyone just yet awhile.'

'I thought now you've had time to consider it, you might have changed your mind. This is our last class. We have the exam next week and then I might never see you again.'

'Well, thanks again for asking. I'm very flattered, but the answer is still no. We'd better go in now or we'll be late.'

Lizzie was aware of him staring at her throughout the class and found it a bit disconcerting. Why didn't he take her word for it when she said no? Still, there was only one more time to come here for the exam and that would be it. She never need see him again, unless of course, she finally landed a job at the Evening Post. She would deal with that when the time came. She refused the invitation to go for coffee and left the others, deciding to walk home on her own. She heard footsteps behind her and walked faster. She glanced behind and saw it was Gregory.

'Wait, Lizzie. I don't like you walking home on your own in the dark. I'll see you back home.'

'I'm fine, Gregory. I've been walking along these roads all my life. Leave me alone.'

'I can't, Lizzie. I love you, Lizzie. You're everything I've ever dreamed of.' He put his arms round her and held her tight. He tried to kiss her, but she fought back and pushed him off.

'Stop it, Gregory,' she almost screeched 'Leave me alone. Go away now or I shall really scream for help.'

He let her go and she relaxed slightly. She felt scared. He was behaving in a very frightening way and a way that she had never experienced before. He grabbed her hand again and tried to pull her back towards him.

She leaned down and bit him. Then as he yelled with shock, she was able to wrench her arm and break right away. She ran off as fast as she could. Luckily she was quite near to her own street and soon arrived back at her door, panting loudly. She banged on the door, too scared to fumble for her key. Ben opened it.

'Lizzie, whatever's happened? Are you all right?' He looked out into the street to see what had scared his little sister so much, but the street was empty. 'Lizzie tell me what happened?'

'It was this chap from my night school. He kept on asking me out and when I said no he followed me.' Her breath was coming out in gulps and she was sobbing between her words. 'He tried to kiss me and held me tightly.'

'Who is he? What does he look like? I'll teach him a lesson he won't forget.' He was grabbing his jacket as he spoke.

'No, Ben. Leave it. But if you can

come and collect me next week after the exam, I'd be very grateful.'

'Course I will, love. But if you tell me who he is, I'll make sure he never comes near you again.'

'Once the exams are over, I'll never have to see him again. Unless I get a job at the Post, of course. I still can't believe they gave that creep the job and not me.'

'You could always write to the Post and complain about him. Or tell the police.'

'Wouldn't do me any good. No, just forget about the wretched Gregory whatever his name is. He seemed all right before, but he just lost control tonight. Mumbled something about loving me. Stupid man clearly doesn't know the meaning of the word.'

'And you do I suppose?'

'I'm not sure. What do you think it means?'

'You're the clever one. Don't ask me.'

'What's going on out there?' Nan yelled from the sitting room. 'Is something wrong?'

'S'all right, Mum. Just taking my coat off.'

'Some lad chased her back and tried to make advances. It's all right. She ran off and I'm taking her and fetching her back next week. Just let him try anything and he'll feel the power of my fist in his face.'

'Oh, love, are you all right?'

'I'm fine, Mum. Don't worry I could run much faster than him.'

'I'll go and put the kettle on. You'll need something to calm you down.'

'And a cup of tea will always do it, I suppose.'

Nellie was worried when Lizzie recounted her evening's adventure, but she was pleased to know that Ben was taking charge for the following week.

There was plenty of work to do so Lizzie didn't have much time to think about the effect of her letter on Charlie or the events of the night before.

After two more days, there had still been nothing from him. Lizzie was getting quite anxious. In her mind, she was thinking he would accept her apology and be round to see her within hours. But it hadn't happened.

She was feeling quite sad and very disappointed. Even the excitement of receiving an offer of payment for her article from the Evening Post did little to cheer her up. She kept willing him to reply before the weekend so they could go out somewhere together on Saturday evening.

'What would you think if Jenny accused you of something you hadn't done?' she asked Ben.

'I'd be furious. It would prove she didn't know me at all.'

'I've made a complete hash of this, haven't I?'

'Looks like it. If you want, you can come out with me and Jenny on Friday. They've got some do on Saturday so she's got Friday off this week.'

'That's nice of you, Ben, but I wouldn't want to play gooseberry. Have you popped the question yet?'

'Course I haven't. You'd know if I had. Why do you ask?'

'I thought you might be going to ask the other week. You seemed all excited about something.'

'I'm thinking of it. But I don't know how it would work cos she's living in at our Nellie's. And she works a lot of evenings. I don't earn enough yet to keep a wife and have somewhere to live.'

'You could always live here. She might change her job anyway. William doesn't need as much looking after now he's bigger. She spends more time as a maid than looking after him. We could have a word with Nellie. See what she thinks.'

'Keep your nose out, smarty-pants. Don't you dare say a word to anyone. Promise?'

'All right. If that's what you want.'

★ ★ ★

The days dragged and still she heard nothing from Charlie. It seemed a long weekend with no outings planned. She couldn't even go to Nellie's on Saturday night as it was one of their dinners. She sat at home with her mother, listening to the radio.

'You could teach me how to sew, Mum. Then I can make some clothes for myself. What do you think?'

'I doubt you'd make much of a seamstress. You're too impatient. Haven't you got one of your books to read? Or you could start on your next article.'

'Bit sad for an eighteen-year-old to be sitting at home on a Saturday.'

By Monday, she was resigned to never hearing from Charlie again. There must be other chaps around. She had already had one request from the awful Gregory so she mustn't be completely unattractive. Nellie was waiting for her in the office.

'I thought I should warn you that Charlie is coming to the factory this morning.'

Lizzie's heart leapt and thumped painfully. 'James wants him to do some new headed paper and also some business cards. If you want to avoid him, he'll be in James's office at ten o'clock. On the other hand, you might want to see him.'

'Oh, Nellie. I don't know what to do. I've never heard a word from him again, even though I wrote him a really nice letter. Do you think he'll ever forgive me? Do you think he'll be horrible to me if I do see him?'

'I really don't know, love. You know him better than I do.'

Lizzie spent the next couple of hours on tenterhooks. She kept looking down the corridor wondering if she might accidentally run into him and then dashed back into safety behind a closed door.

When she heard a man's footsteps along the corridor and a knock at James's office door, she was certain he was here. How long might he be in with James? She resumed her peering into the corridor and heard James's door open. Clutching a file, she went into the corridor and straight out in front of Charlie.

'Lizzie. How are you?'

'Charlie. How nice to see you. Have you been to see James?'

'Mr Cobridge has placed a further order with me.'

'Oh, that's good. Erm, did you get my letter?' she asked, slightly dreading his answer.

'Yes, thank you. I'm glad my name was cleared.'

'I'm really sorry I doubted you. I don't know what came over me.'

'I dare say you were upset at the time. Not a nice thing to happen, though. Well, I must get back to the shop. Good bye.'

'Charlie . . . can't we still be friends?'

'Friends? I'm really not sure. Besides, you have a new *friend* now, don't you?'

'What? What on earth do you mean?'

'I came round to your street one evening, hoping to see you to sort things out. You were kissing someone. A younger man than me.'

'Are you sure you weren't mistaken? I've never kissed anyone else.'

'You were certainly wrapped up in someone's arms.'

'Oh, my goodness. Gregory. You must have seen that odious young man, Gregory. He tried to kiss me once and then the next time followed me home and tried again. I bit him and escaped.' Charlie's mouth widened to a grin.

'You bit him?'

'Well yes. It was easier than fighting him. He was stronger than me.' She almost smiled herself and then relaxed into a giggle at the sight of his face. He was stifling his own laughter.

'Remind me not to get into a fight with you. That's fighting dirty!'

'Oh, Charlie, I have really missed you.'

'I've missed you too, but I'm still having trouble knowing you could believe I would be dishonest. You were too quick to accuse without finding out the facts. I understand that your brother-in-law knew immediately who

251

was the real culprit.'

'Well yes, partly. He knows the main person behind it. The manufacturer. There's still someone among the workers who passed out actual drawings.'

'Difficult. Well, as I said, I must get back. I'm glad we cleared the air.'

'Does this mean we can go out together again?'

'Maybe. I'll give it some thought. Though it might be a bit scary knowing you bite.'

'Only when I'm scared. You'll just have to make sure you don't frighten me.'

He left, without making any arrangements to see her again. It was disappointing but at least they were speaking again. Strange that he just happened to be in their road when Gregory made his attempt to kiss her. What rotten luck that he should think the worst of her. But maybe, they were quits now.

When she arrived home on Friday

after work, there was a note waiting for her. It had been delivered by hand.

'Oh, it's from Charlie. He's asking if I'd like to go out with him tomorrow night. Oh Mum, isn't that great news?'

'If that's what you want, love, of course it is.'

'Oh, it is. I really do want to go. I have to telephone to let him know my answer. Oh dear, I'll have to go to Nellie's to make a call. Why can't we get a telephone put in here? I wish you'd agree to it.'

'Horrible things. Ringing when you don't them to. No thanks. I decided I don't want one of them. Not at all. I've heard how it goes off, interrupting everything when I've been at Nellie's. And they've got people to answer it for them.'

'I think you're wrong. Not many people will ever want to telephone us, but it would save an awful lot of walking round to Nellie's. Besides, you're getting on a bit now and if you're not well, how are you going to let anyone know?'

'Well, thanks a lot. I'm not that ancient. I'll think about it. But if I move to Nellie's it would have been a waste of money.'

'I thought you'd given up on that idea.'

'I have a bit. There's no sign of you moving out and I expect if Ben does ask Jenny to marry him, they'll want to live here.'

'I see. I'm going to phone Charlie. Don't bother to keep anything for me for tea. I'll have something at Nellie's.'

In the end, there was no meal being served at Cobridge House. Jenny was going out for a meal with Ben and Nellie and James were also dining out.

She made her telephone call and arranged that Charlie would pick her up from home at seven the following day. He also suggested they had a meal out so there would be chance to talk properly. She felt slightly nervous as she had only ever eaten at Nellie's, apart from home. Still, James did everything very properly, so she expected she would know the right cutlery to use and what different foods were.

On impulse, the next morning, she went to the hairdressers and ordered the stylist to cut her hair short.

'Are you sure madam? Only you've got such lovely curls. I'd kill to have hair like that and such a beautiful shade. Sort of light copper, isn't it?'

'I suppose so but it gets so messy. Takes ages to dry when I wash it. I'm really sick of it like this. What I'd really like is one of these sleek modern styles with a sort of bob that curls under, but that won't work. Oh well, all right then. Cut it a lot shorter so I don't have to tie it back all the time, but not as short as I said at first. I don't want it to look all bushy.'

'I'll see what I can do. You'll never get it looking straight and sleek. Just think of all the ladies who come in here wanting curls. Nobody ever seems happy with what they've got. So, you going somewhere special?'

The stylist was well practised in idle chit chat and Lizzie was glad when it was all over. She was quite pleased with the result but she still wished for one of the fashionable straighter styles.

'Golly, you look different,' Charlie exclaimed when he called for her. 'It is still Lizzie under there, is it?'

'You hate it, don't you?' she said miserably.

'I don't hate it. It was just a shock. No, I quite like it. In fact, you look lovely. Is that a new dress?'

'As usual, new to me. Nellie never keeps her clothes for very long so they are never worn out. James always insists she looks smart for every event. I think when they were first married, she always told him there was plenty of wear in her clothes and refused to buy new ones. Lucky for me she changed her mind.'

'Come on then. We'll have to catch a bus. We're going up to Newcastle. There's a new restaurant opened there and I'm told it's very good so I've booked a table.'

They were seated by a man wearing what Lizzie thought must be an evening dress suit. He shook out a starched white napkin and placed it on her knee. She felt like giggling, but managed to stifle it.

He handed her a menu that was almost like a small poster and which was covered in fancy writing on both sides. She glanced at Charlie to see how he was coping. He winked at her and started to read the menu.

'Did you do French at school?'

'Yes, I did.'

'So do you know what the heck all this is about?'

'Turn it over and it's written in English. Bit posh all this, isn't it?'

'I wanted this evening to be special.'

'It certainly is different. I've never been anywhere like this before. The most eating out I've done, is in the cafeteria in the big stores. Oh, and the café when we've had coffee after night school.'

'I'm going to have the soup and then I fancy a steak. What do you feel like?'

'I'll have the same. What's this garlic stuff with the steak like?'

'I have no idea. We'll find out together.'

It was a lovely evening and by the end of it, Lizzie felt that she was finally forgiven and discovered she liked garlic! They caught the last bus home and he put his arm round her waist as they walked back to her house.

'Am I allowed to kiss you?' he asked.

'You'd better or I shall think I'm still in the dog house.'

'Oh Lizzie, I have missed you. I realise just how much after this evening.'

'I know. I was trying to work out what love is and whether I love you.' She felt him stiffen slightly as she used the dreaded word. 'Don't worry. I didn't really work it out. I just knew that I'd be desperately upset if I didn't see you again. It would be like a bereavement.'

He smiled down at her. He was a nice, four inches taller than her and it made her feel sort of cared for and protected.

'I don't want to rush you into anything, but I think I have decided that I do know what love is. I love you, Lizzie. I love you a lot and I also know that it's you I'd like to spend my life with.'

'Oh, my goodness. Is that almost a proposal?'

'Well, I suppose it is. But I know you have ambitions. I know you want a career and I'll be the last person to get in the way of that.'

'Yes, Charlie.'

'I know you do. It's all right. As I said, I'm not rushing you into anything.'

'I meant yes, if it was a proposal, I'm saying, yes. As long as we don't start having babies and I can have a career as well. I want too much, don't I?'

'Not necessarily. But, we do need to think carefully. Make sure we have things properly planned before we take this leap. You haven't even met my parents yet.'

She shivered, not at the prospect of meeting Mr and Mrs Swift but because she was starting to feel cold. 'Sorry, we shouldn't be standing out here talking. Why don't you come to our house for tea tomorrow and you can meet my parents then.'

'Won't they mind? I mean it's rather short notice.'

'It won't bother them. I'm not sure what we shall eat, but that doesn't matter. It's the meeting that's the important thing. You should know, my dad's pretty immobile. He needs a lot of help. He likes to be involved in the business, but only in a minor way. I leave him to check through the books and even write invoices, but he's not able to concentrate for long.'

'And how's your mum?'

'Not too good either. I have to do all the shopping and some of the cooking.'

'Oh Charlie, you do have to work hard.'

'I'm used to it. I'll come and pick you up about half-past two, if that suits. Now, get yourself inside before you freeze.'

'Thanks for a lovely evening. And let's not tell anyone we're making plans for the future. Not yet awhile. Let's keep it to ourselves.'

'I think that's a very good idea. Night, Lizzie.' He kissed her again and with a warm glow, she felt as if she was floating.

'You look happy, love. I take it you had a good evening and made up with Charlie again?'

'Yes, Mum. It was wonderful. A really posh restaurant with a proper French chef. I ate garlic on a steak. It's amazing. Like onion only well, a lot different and much more concentrated.'

'I wondered what the smell was.'

'You mean I smell?'

'You do a bit.'

'But Charlie ate it too and he didn't smell.'

'Maybe if you both eat it, you don't notice it.'

'I won't ever eat it again. What a shame. I liked it. By the way, I'm going to meet his parents tomorrow. For tea. I'm really tired now so I'll see you in the morning. Night.'

'Don't you want a cup of tea?' Nan called to the closing door. 'I assume not.'

Lizzie just wanted to be alone. She lay on her bed, thinking about the evening. Engaged. Just imagine, she was engaged to Charlie. She laughed in sheer delight and hugged her arms round herself.

Only her and Charlie knew. And she was going to meet his parents tomorrow. That was a bit scary but if they were half as nice as Charlie, there could be no problem. She hoped.

'You'd Better Call
The Police'

Lizzie spent much of the morning speculating about the afternoon to come. She went through her usual crisis of what to wear. Smart but not too smart. Would Charlie's parents like her? She made up her mind not to be too talkative or sound too full of her own importance. Nan wished her well as she was leaving and hoped she had a nice time.

'I'll be at Nellie's this afternoon, as usual. Make sure you've got your door key with you if you get back before me.'

'Thanks, Mum. Have a nice time and give my love to everyone.'

★ ★ ★

'I hope you're not expecting too much. My parents aren't really like your

263

family. They're quiet and a bit reserved. But if they don't say much, you mustn't worry that they don't like you. It's just their way,' Charlie told her as they approached his home.

'What have you told them about me? I mean, you haven't said anything about us probably getting engaged?'

'I didn't realise it was a 'probably'. I thought you'd said yes?'

'I did. I mean yes. But it won't feel like it's definite until we have an engagement ring.'

'Then everyone will know.'

'Oh, I don't know. Yes. We'll consider us engaged and one day soon, cos I won't be able to keep it to myself, we'll tell everyone.'

'Oh, Lizzie, Lizzie. You are funny. I do love you.'

'There. You said it in daylight. Let me look at your face when you say it.' She stopped walking and looked at him. He repeated his words and looked at her very tenderly.

'Oh Charlie, you really do mean it,

don't you? Ooh I'm the happiest girl in the whole of the Potteries.'

They reached the printing shop and he unlocked a small door at the side. It led into a narrow passage with a flight of steps at the end.

'We could have gone through the shop, but this is really the main entrance to our place,' he told her. 'My parents are not well, as I've told you, so don't be disappointed if you don't seem to get much of a welcome. They're not used to having visitors these days.' He opened the door and called out to his parents.

The sitting room was quite small and rather dark. It was full of furniture and every shelf was covered in items of pottery, brass or faded photographs in fussy frames. Mr Swift was seated in a large armchair near the fire, while his wife perched on the edge of a chair near the table.

'Mum, Dad, this is Lizzie. The friend I told you about.'

'Hello, dear. Are you the young lady

who was at school with Charlie?'

'Pleased to meet you, Mrs Swift. No, we weren't at school together.' She looked at Charlie who shook his head, indicating she should say no more.

'Don't be daft, Elsie. You can see she's much younger than our lad. Come and sit down, love. Don't take much notice of Elsie. She's, well she gets confused these days.'

'Thank you. Pleased to meet you too, Mr Swift.'

'If you'll excuse me for a minute or two, I'll go and put the kettle on,' Charlie said.

'Can I help?' Lizzie asked slightly desperately. She didn't want to be left with these two slightly odd strangers.

'If you like. I've made some sandwiches and there's a sponge cake. Not homemade like you're used to, I'm afraid.'

'I bet it will taste wonderful. I always used to think it was a real treat to have shop-bought cake, like I said in the park that day. Now, what can I do?'

'There's a tablecloth in the drawer there. If you could take the bits and pieces off the table, you can spread it over there. Just ignore anything Mum says. She might ask you, well just about anything really.'

'Does she have some sort of problem?' Lizzie asked before she could stop herself.

'She's just a bit confused at times.'

She took the tablecloth and smiled at Charlie's parents as she moved a vase and several other items from the table. She spread the cloth and smiled again, being unable to think of what to say. It wasn't like her at all. She felt a bit of an idiot really, but she smiled at the couple and escaped back into the kitchen. He was loading teacups and plates onto a tray and had a plate of sandwiches ready to take through. They set everything out on the table.

'Are you going to sit at the table, Dad, or do you want me to pass things over to you?'

'I'll stay here, thanks, lad. Easier than

getting up. I'm a bit stiff in my joints, you understand,' he explained to Lizzie.

'That must be difficult for you,' she said. 'Can I pass you something?'

'Just put a couple of sandwiches on a plate. Ta, love.'

Conversation was somewhat stilted and it seemed a rather long afternoon. Lizzie and Charlie exchanged a few smiles as they ate the simple meal.

He was definitely in charge of things and she could see that his parents were totally reliant on him. She began to feel rather uncomfortable as thoughts of their possible future began to dawn on her.

They couldn't manage without their son to do everything for them. If she and Charlie were to get married, she could be the one looking after everyone. How could she possibly have a career, if that was the case? This could be quite some dilemma she would have to address. It was not a prospect she would relish.

Being the youngest child in the

family, she had never had younger siblings to help with and she admitted, she had probably been spoilt by her brothers and especially Nellie. Caring for someone else was not in her nature, particularly anyone not part of her close family. She loved Charlie, she was sure, but would she ever cope with being part of this home situation?

Once tea was over, Lizzie suggested they should wash the dishes together.

'I couldn't let you do that. You're a guest.'

'It's all right. You'd only have to do it on your own later, so let's get on with it.'

'Well, if you're sure you don't mind. Wash or dry?'

'Dry. Then I won't splash myself.'

'I'm sorry if you're disappointed that they don't talk much.'

'Don't be daft. It's how they are. I happen to come from a noisy family. Perhaps they'll be better when they know me a bit more.'

'I doubt it. They're always like this.

When my uncle comes round, that's Mum's brother, they don't say much then, either.'

'It must be very difficult for you. You have to do such a lot for them.'

'It's got worse since Dad stopped moving around so much. He can't get down the stairs now so he's stuck up here all the time. I've been suggesting we try to get them a bungalow or ground floor flat somewhere so they can be on one level. But Mum doesn't want anything to change. She likes things the way they are.'

The discussion went on and once they had finished the dishes, Charlie put him arms round his girl.

'Thanks very much for coming round. I hope it hasn't put you off me too much.'

'Thank you for inviting me.' She hedged her words carefully.

'I'll walk you home. Just in case the strange Gregory is lurking anywhere. Need to keep you safe.'

'Hopefully I'll never have to see him

again after my exam on Tuesday evening.'

They said goodbye to Mr and Mrs Swift and slowly walked back to Lizzie's home. She had a number of thoughts racing round her brain, not least among them how the care Charlie gave to his parents would work out when, or if they were to marry. She dreaded the prospect of having to cope with anything like that.

'You're worrying about my parents, aren't you?' Charlie said at last after they had walked in silence for a while.

'I didn't realise they depended on you quite so much. How do they manage when you aren't there?'

'Mum can do some things herself. And so can Dad. He just gets a bit lazy at times. If I'm going out for the evening or an afternoon, I leave things ready for them.'

'You're marvellous, Charlie. I don't think I'd be any good at all. You don't have any brothers or sisters to help you?'

'I'm an only one. Pluses and minuses I suppose. Like I said, I shall have to get them to move one of these days. It's a ridiculous situation. Anyway, enough of me. Tell me about your exam. What will you have to do?'

By the time Lizzie had recounted what she was expecting in the way of shorthand tests, they had reached her street. The lights were on in the house so at least there was someone in. Someone she might be able to talk to. They said their goodbyes and Lizzie reached up to kiss him goodbye.

'Thank you very much for having me. I'll look forward to next weekend. It will be nice to have a whole day out on Saturday.' Charlie had suggested they took the bus to Trentham Gardens, a large park area of pleasure gardens and other attractions.

'I'll see you on Saturday at ten o'clock. And good luck for your exam.' He watched as she went inside and turned to go home.

He had delayed taking her to meet

his parents, fearing it would put her off, but having discussed marriage at some future time, he knew she needed to be put in the picture. He simply didn't know how he would cope if his parents refused to move. His life was tough enough with running the business and looking after them.

They did own the shop and living accommodation outright and the business was now making a reasonable profit so they could probably afford somewhere more suitable for themselves and get in some sort of help. But his mother was difficult and too set in her ways. He sighed and prayed that Lizzie would be able to come to terms with it.

Ben was home when she went inside. He was sitting by the fire, deep in thought.

'Hello. Mum not back yet?'

'No. She was staying on for supper with Nellie. James is out again. Some meeting or other.'

'James is out on his own an awful lot lately.'

'Maybe. Lizzie, can I talk to you?'

'Thought we were talking.'

'I mean in confidence. You're a girl and you're friends with Jenny. I want to ask her to marry me, but I don't know how to go about it and what we can do about having a home together.'

'Just ask her right out, is how to go about it. The other thing is tricky. We said before, she lives in at Nellie's and some of her work is at night anyway. Maybe Nellie would let you have a room there?'

'I couldn't do that. I'd hate it and I doubt James would allow it any road. Well, I don't think he would.'

'Could you afford to live if Jenny wasn't working?'

'Well, I suppose so, but what would she do with herself? I've got a bit of savings, but by the time we'd got somewhere to live and got furniture and everything, there'd be nothing left.'

They discussed various options, including moving in to their home with Nan. There was space enough but it didn't get round Jenny's work problem.

'Maybe you need to discuss it with Nellie. You'd best ask Jenny first of course. If she says no, it's all academic anyway.'

'How do you mean?'

'If she says no, there's nothing to discuss.'

'Do you reckon she'll say no, then?'

'Not at all. I think she really wants to marry you. You're not bad looking when you get scrubbed up. You've got a steady job as long as Cobridge's are still in business.'

'What? Have you heard the rumours then?'

'Nellie and James say there's nothing to them.'

'And you believe them?'

'Why wouldn't I? What have you heard?'

'The lads down our end say there's talk of merging with another company cos the order books are empty. That Brown company copied our new lines and that was what everyone was pinning their hopes on.'

'Is there someone down your end who sounds as if they know a bit too much? We still don't know who took the designs out.'

'There's one chap who's courting one of the girls in your decorating shop. He always seems to know what's going on. They get together at dinner times and they always seem to be close together whispering about something. We tease him all the time about . . . well you know how blokes are.'

'So who are these two?'

'Alf Ainsley and someone called Mary. I don't know her other name'

'I think I know her. She's a very good paintress, but she's been here for years, I think. She has been working on the new stuff. How long has Alf been there?'

'Came to us from Wedgewood's when they moved out to Barlaston, I think. All very nice having a modern place like that in the country, but it's too far to go to work when you live the other side of town. Any road, what's this got to do with me and my problems?'

'Sorry, Ben. Nothing really, but you've given me something to pass on to Nellie and James. Ideas anyway. But as for your problems as you put it, you'd better talk to Jenny next. Thought you might have seen her this afternoon?'

'She was busy so I came home on my own. I'm seeing her on Tuesday night.'

'Oh, the night you're seeing me back from my exam? Thanks very much.'

'Crikey. I'd forgotten. I suppose we could walk round to the centre and then all walk back together.'

'And I could watch you make a mess of proposing to Jenny? No thanks. I'll sort something else. Charlie might be able to come and walk me home.'

'Oh yes. It was the big 'meet the parents day', wasn't it? How did that go?'

'Oh don't. My turn to talk to you now. I want you to swear you won't say a word of this to Mum or anyone?' He looked puzzled, but he nodded and made the cross my heart sign.

'Charlie has to look after his parents. His dad is all right, but he's immobile. Can't walk properly. His mother is really strange. She hardly says anything at all and does nothing all day, as far as I can make out.'

'Blimey. You'd never guess it looking at Charlie. He's a good bloke. We're all wondering if he's going to pop the question.' Lizzie blushed and looked away. 'Hey, little sister he has, hasn't he? Go on, tell me, did you say yes?'

'Not a word to anyone? Right?' Ben nodded again, a grin on his face. 'I did sort of say yes, but now I'm worried about how I'd cope with his parents. They refuse to move out to a flat or something where they could get about better.'

'I thought you were looking pleased with yourself this morning. Maybe you and Charlie could get somewhere of your own when you're wed?'

'Maybe, but they need him. He does

everything for them.'

'I can see your worries. You never did strike me as a Florence Nightingale type.'

'Besides, they live above his printing business. He has to be there most of the time for work.'

They heard Nan's key in the door and both stopped talking.

'Not a word. Promise?' Lizzie hissed.

'Nor you.'

'Hello, you two. You've nearly let the fire out. Doesn't anyone ever do anything in this place without me?'

'Course not, Mum. We'd never dare.'

As she lay in bed, thinking through the recent events, Lizzie decided that falling in love made life very complicated. Before she met Charlie, she slept well, ate well and only had to worry about her school exams or getting a job.

Now everything seemed to bring problems. She had been so concerned with it all after she and Charlie broke up briefly, she hadn't even done anything more about her articles for the Evening Post.

Perhaps she should try to think about that and forget all this emotional stuff. She must remember to tell Nellie about the connection between Mary and this Alf person, that Ben had mentioned.

Nellie was unwilling to believe that Mary could be involved with any of this passing on of designs.

'She's a good worker and she has been with us for a couple of years. I've always trusted her.'

'But she's only been going out with Alf for a few weeks. Don't you think he might have influenced her in some way?'

'Possible I suppose. I might get Vera to do some digging. Now, I need some letters writing. I'll give you some more shorthand practice.'

They worked together well. Having had the better education, Lizzie was able to phrase things a little more correctly at times. Nellie never commented, but she realised how much she was beginning to rely on her sister. She would miss her if she did leave to work on the local paper.

'Do you mind if I telephone Charlie? Only I'm hoping he'll come and walk me home after my exam tomorrow. I don't want to walk on my own and Ben is going out with Jenny.'

'I'll come and pick you up in the car. It's not like you to be afraid of walking back on your own. Oh, that lad from your class. I'd forgotten for a minute. Perhaps you should put a complaint in to the police.'

'I don't want him to get into trouble with the law. It was just a one time thing, but I didn't like it. I think he's quite harmless really. Anyway, thanks. I finish at half-past eight if you can come to get me.'

Lizzie did the typing and listened as Nellie interviewed Vera about the possible leak in security.

'Elsie and Babs would never do anything wrong. I wouldn't have thought Mary would either. OK. I'll see what I can find out about this Alf Ainsley. If she wanted to impress a new boyfriend, she might be tempted.'

Nellie cursed. She had enough to do without playing detective. 'I've got too much to do without all this stuff,' she muttered.

'Why don't I go down there and do some prying?' Lizzie offered. 'I can always do a bit of flirting with the lads. Someone might let something slip.'

'Be careful, love. All right you can go. Ask the casting manager how the numbers are going. Here, take this list with you. It'll make it look legitimate. They're due a tea break soon so hang around and listen to the gossip. Our Ben is always around so you can always chat to him for a bit. Thanks, love. I don't know what I'd ever do without you. You've made a big difference to me having you work here.'

'Thanks, Nellie. That's nice of you to say so. But . . . '

'I know. You don't want to be here forever. You still want to be a writer.'

She went to the clay department and watched fascinated as the various machines pressed lumps of clay onto moulds and proper looking plates were released. The new squarer shapes had involved new machine parts and she hadn't seen them working. The manager saw her and came over.

'Can I help?'

She used the cover story and he went to his office to get the figures. Suddenly, the machines were stopped and the workers reached for their mugs. A young lad appeared with a vast teapot and started pouring a yellowish liquid which had already had milk and sugar added. It looked horrible to Lizzie's eyes.

'Hello, gorgeous. Are you coming to join us,' one of the men called out. She saw Ben stepping forward and she winked at him to keep away.

'Just wanted to see how you're all getting on. Don't get down here very often.'

'Heart and soul of the factory. So

what's your name?' asked a dark haired lad.

'Don't you know her?' another one said. 'She's Mr James's sister-in-law. Lizzie, isn't it?'

'I see. Bit too posh to be with the likes of us then. I'm Alf. Pleased to meet you.' He held out a white, clay covered hand. She smiled and shook it.

'Haven't seen you around before. You new then?'

'Last three months. They discovered they can't manage without me. So, are you courting then?'

'Hands off, lad. She's not for the likes of us. Besides, aren't you spoken for, Alf? The lovely Mary will be down later. You don't want her to catch you flirting with one of the bosses.'

'So, where were you working before?' Lizzie asked as casually as she could.

'Wedgewood's for a bit. Then some other places. Plenty of experience.'

'So why didn't you stay there, if you're as good as you say?'

He frowned and glared at her.

'What's it to you?' His voice was edgy and he had a curl to his lips that was most unpleasant to look at.

'Nothing at all. Just interested to know about you all. Ah, here's the manager with the figures I was after.'

'You've got a good enough figure of your own. Shouldn't worry about any other figures, pretty girl like you.'

She grinned, took the sheet of paper and waved goodbye to them all. They were a cheery lot on the whole, but she had taken an instant dislike to Alf. She needed to know exactly where he had worked before. His records would be in James's secretary's office.

She went straight there and wiped the clay off her hands before knocking at the door. The secretary wasn't too happy about letting the girl see the confidential records about one of the workers. When Lizzie explained, she unlocked the filing cabinet and took out his file. She saw the evidence. He had worked for Brown's for a few weeks after leaving the Wedgewood factory.

'Do you have to get references for everyone when they join us?'

'Of course. But we don't always keep them. Some of them have written papers from previous employers, sort of testimonials that belong to them. We usually write to ask for something more formal. There will be a letter from Mr Brown in there.'

'Thanks very much. You've answered a number of questions for me.'

She could hardly wait to get back to tell Nellie what she had discovered. Alf had a record of working for Brown's and he had a girlfriend in this department. Though it was too late to recover the stolen designs from the first collection, the newest ones might still be safe. They put Vera on the case and she was scrutinising each girl, especially Mary, as they left for the day.

'Can I look at your paper, love?' Vera asked innocently. 'Only I saw you reading it earlier and thought you might have finished with it.'

Mary looked uncomfortable and blushed scarlet.

'I have to take it home for my dad,' she said bundling it into her bag.

'That's fine. Will you lend it me for a mo'? I'd like to read my horoscope. See if the tall handsome stranger's going to take me out for supper.'

'You can't,' said the girl, near to tears.

'And why would that be? Is there something hidden in there? Something you don't want me to see?'

Mary collapsed. She slumped down into a chair and sobbed. Vera took the newspaper and opened it to find the design pages she knew were hidden in there. Mary sobbed again.

'I told him I'd get found out. But he said he'd punish me if I didn't. Make my face a mess so nobody would ever look at me again.'

'And you really want to be with someone like that?'

'He's good to me most of the time. Buys me lovely presents and takes me dancing and everything.'

'You silly girl. You're in terrible trouble, you know. They'll have to call the police and everything. Now stay sitting where you are and don't move.'

'But I have to get home or my dad'll be mad at me if I haven't got his tea ready.'

'Bad luck. You stay there till I get Mrs Nellie.' Vera turned to the office and waved at Nellie to come. Lizzie went into the decorating shop with her sister and they listened as Vera explained.

'Lizzie. Phone the gatehouse and get George to stop Alf leaving. Then ring his office to fetch Mr James down here. We'll let him decide if the police are to be called. And you lot,' she said to the collection of girls standing round watching, 'can all get yourselves home. If any of you live near Mary, you'd better tell her dad that she won't be home for a bit.'

'I wouldn't dare,' Elsie said. 'He's a bad tempered old . . . oh, poor Mary. She's a silly girl who's had it rough since her mum died. Alf made her think she was special, but we all suspected he was using her for his own rotten dealings. Go easy on her if you possibly can, Mrs Nellie. She isn't a bad girl. She's had it tough.'

'No promises, but I'll take your comments on board.'

Lizzie answered the phone when it rang.

'George has got Alf down there at the gate house. He can't leave his post as he still has to check everyone else out.'

'I'll go and fetch him myself,' Nellie said. She was at boiling point with rage.

'Will you be all right?' Lizzie asked anxiously.

'You stay here with Mary. I'll go with Nellie,' Vera said. She was a fairly large woman and had a commanding presence. Lizzie nodded and the two women went off. She picked up the phone again and called James's secretary.

'Can you ask Mr James to come to Nellie's office please. It's urgent.' Mary was still sitting where she had been told. 'You'd better come into the office,' she said and the girl followed her, now totally cowed.

Poor girl, Lizzie thought. She's obviously never had a chance. Shame, as she was turning into a talented worker. It seemed an age before anyone returned, but then James arrived and Lizzie put him in the picture.

Mary cringed down in her seat, red-eyed and her nose runny. She was the very picture of misery. At last, Nellie and Vera came back, escorting a defiant Alf.

'You can't pin nothin' on me,' he was protesting. 'You snivelling little snitch,' he said as he saw Mary sitting there. 'You're a grass. A miserable grass.'

'I think the police will be having words with you. It's all your idea, isn't it? How much did Brown's pay you?'

'I'm not admitting to owt.' He sat on the edge of the desk and clamped his jaws shut.

'You'd better call the police, please,

Lizzie. We'll let them sort it out. Can you stay with them till the police arrive?' he asked the three women. 'I'll be back in a minute. Just have to finish something.'

* * *

'So there we were, me leaning against the door to stop anyone leaving,' Lizzie told her mother and Ben over supper. 'It was just like one of them thrillers at the pictures. Any road, the police came and took them in. We all had to sign statements and so that's why I was so late getting home.'

'So what's going to happen now?'

'I think James was talking about suing Brown's and Alf will probably end up in jail. It's not his only crime. Don't know about Mary. Poor girl gets it from all sides. Her dad slaps her and so did Alf. We saw some of her bruises. She's been let out of the police station, but Alf's been kept in 'til he appears in court tomorrow. Exciting stuff, eh?'

'I only hope you sleep after all the excitement. You need to be on top form for your exam. Oh, you never told me how you got on at Charlie's yesterday?'

'It was all right. They're very quiet people so I didn't really get to know them much. But they're nice enough,' she fibbed.

'P'raps you'd like to invite them round here for tea one day? What do you think?' Nan suggested.

'I doubt they'd come. They don't go out much. But thanks anyway and I'll tell Charlie you asked. We're going to Trentham Gardens for the day on Saturday.'

'How lovely. I've heard it's very nice there. There was stuff in the Evening Post when the swimming pool was opened. Bit chilly for that at this time of year.'

The next day at the factory, the story of Alf and Mary was the only topic of conversation. Mary didn't come in and the girls were speculating as to whether she'd been sacked. Nellie hadn't quite decided yet, as she believed the girl had been totally coerced into it by her so-called boyfriend. Her absence left a gap on the bench and there was no-one else available to fill it.

'To think James has been negotiating with Abraham Brown as a possible merger. We need to invest in new processes and the only way we can afford it is to merge with another company. We even entertained the man in our own home.'

'I didn't much like him when I was playing at being a waitress. So, where do we go from here?'

'Don't know. James met with a couple of other people on Sunday night. They had dinner somewhere and he seemed quite cheerful when he got home. He never says very much about his dealings. Now, are you all ready for tonight? If you want to go home early to get ready, I'm happy with that.'

The exam was over quickly and the others all planned to go and celebrate afterwards.

'Come on Lizzie. We might never meet again.'

'I'm getting a lift home so I can't, but thanks for asking me. Good luck, everyone. I hope you all pass with flying colours.' Ironically, Gregory hadn't turned up for the exam so she needn't have worried about his unwelcome attentions. 'Wonder what happened to Gregory?' she said to the others.

'Oh, he gave up. I heard he'd got the sack from the paper so he decided it wasn't worth coming.'

'Really? Wonder why?'

'I think he was being too pushy with one of the secretaries and she reported him to the boss. He happened to choose the wrong person to try anything on. He was a funny lad.'

'Tell me about it. That's my sister's car now. Cheerio, everyone. Hope you all do well.'

'Bye, Lizzie. Good luck.'

'Thanks for coming to collect me, Nellie. That awful Gregory wasn't there tonight. Evidently, he's been sacked from the Evening Post. I'm wondering if they'll offer his job to me. They did say they'd let me know when there's a vacancy.'

'That's nice for you,' Nellie said in a flat voice. 'Like I said before, I was hoping you were settling in with us at Cobridge's, but I know you've always had ambitions to write.'

Lizzie smiled in the darkness. She was pleased to be appreciated, but if a job was offered, she could hardly refuse it. 'Nearly there. I'll pop in for a few minutes to see Mum. I worry about her being on her own so much. It's not good for her.'

'She never has been one for going out much.'

'She used to go to chapel meetings much more often than she does now. Don't you remember her organising all those outings and everything? It was the Sunday School Anniversary last week and she didn't even go to see the kids doing their recitations and everything. She used to love it so.'

'And we all hated it. She made us learn something for it every year, didn't she?' They sat in the car reminiscing for several minutes.

'Oh, how lovely to see you, Nellie. What are you doing here?'

'Thought I'd give Lizzie a lift home after her exam and I'd just pop in to see you.'

'That was nice of you. How did it go, love?'

'All right, I think. Shall I put the kettle on?'

'Our Ben not in?' Nellie asked. 'Oh no, of course not. He was going out with Jenny. Up to something, I suspect. What do you think, Lizzie?'

'How should I know?' She crossed her fingers behind her back to cancel the fib. She put the kettle on and wondered how things were going for her brother. She felt quite excited to think he and Jenny might soon be engaged. She hoped Nellie would give them a little party like she had done with Joe and Daisy. Be nice if she and

Charlie could also announce their news, but she was now having serious doubts about that possibility. Maybe she should talk it through with her sister.

'Does anyone want anything to eat with the tea? Only I'm starving. Is there still some cake left, Mum?'

'There's a couple of slices in the tin. I sometimes think you've got hollow legs, our Lizzie. And you always stay so skinny.'

'Nellie works me so hard I never have time to eat at the factory.'

They all laughed together. It was a warm, family feeling and one Lizzie remembered from being a child.

'I'm so lucky to have you two in my family,' she said suddenly, feeling almost tearful.

She knew that Charlie had never known a family closeness like this and could never have felt the same sort of affection for his own parents. Perhaps this was something she could bring to him if they were married. She had a large family she could share with him.

Decisions Must Be Made

When Ben finally arrived home, he had a soppy grin on his face, according to Lizzie the next day when she was telling Nellie that he had proposed to Jenny and she had accepted.

'I'm not surprised,' was the reaction. 'They've both been wandering round in a sort of pink haze for the last few weeks. Do you know what their plans are?'

'Not sure. I think he was going to talk it through with you. Ben's a bit worried that they won't be able to manage on just his wages and any road, Jenny doesn't want to let you down with little William and all. Bit tricky with her living in.'

'I'll have to have a think and see what he suggests when he comes to have this talk. Thanks for putting me in the picture anyway. What did Mum say?'

'She was really pleased. Wants to get all her little chicks settled. She did say they could both live at home for a bit, anyway.'

'I really wanted her to come and live here with us. I think she's got quite lonely. She's not getting about much these days either. Just have to get you sorted out and then we're all set. What are you thinking of doing with your future? You get everyone else sorted but not yourself.'

'I don't really know. I've been thinking a lot about working at the paper, but I know I'd just be a dogsbody there. If I can sell some articles, it means I'd still be writing the sort of things that interest me and if I stay here working for you, I'd have a steady wage. And I've also been thinking about that children's book.

'You know, the one based on the stories you used to tell me. The fairy plates could be used as the pictures and we might sell more of those. Do other stuff too, to go with the pictures in the book. Plates and beakers using small parts of the design. I might do stuff for boys as well and we could make beakers and dishes to sell along with them. Things about trains or tractors or anything else they like.'

'I think this all sounds splendid. A real marketing opportunity. We must discuss it in detail. If it means you'll stay here, I should be delighted. Oh Lizzie, you'd make me so happy. Someone working here for me, that I can completely trust and rely on.'

'I know, Nellie, and I'm flattered, but I haven't really made the decision. If they offered me a job on the Evening Post I still might feel I have to try it. I was really just thinking aloud.' Nellie's smile faded, but she nodded her agreement and settled to her working day. There were so many things to consider for everyone.

Ben was delighted that Jenny had agreed to marry him and that was enough for him for the time being. He didn't want to make plans for an actual wedding for a few months so they were happy to continue life as an engaged couple.

Nellie organised an engagement party for the family and included all the staff at Cobridge House the following Sunday. Though the cook had prepared the food, the maids and everyone came to eat together and Lizzie and her mother happily helped serve and clear up afterwards.

The only person who wasn't at ease, was James. He was very much the outsider at the party, despite or perhaps because of being the house owner. He made his escape as soon as he felt it to be decent. Everyone relaxed after this and Nellie felt it was quite like old times, when she had been part of the household staff.

'So Lizzie,' said Ethel, the oldest of the maids, 'we just have to get you settled and it's full house. Where's that young man of yours, today? Are you still seeing each other?'

'Oh, yes. We spent yesterday at Trentham Gardens. It's so lovely there.

We should organise a day out there for everyone next spring, Nellie.'

'Oh yes, what a good idea. A treat for all our staff here at Cobridge House. I've heard it's lovely.'

'We could get up a coach party. Take a picnic.'

Lizzie was pleased the attention was deflected from her and Charlie as everyone began planning the outing, despite it being months in advance. Nellie asked her later if things were all right with her and Charlie.

'He'd have been very welcome to come here today,' she said.

'Oh, I know but we were out all day yesterday and his parents needed him.'

The party drew to a close after nine o'clock. Jenny came to Nellie and shyly thanked her for a lovely celebration.

'My pleasure. You'll be one of the family soon so of course, we were pleased to do it. We'll have a talk about the future soon. Make sure we all know what we should do for the best. Don't worry, I'm sure we can manage something. We'll decide where you need to live and we'll help you find somewhere.' Jenny was almost in tears of joy and gratitude.

A letter arrived from the Evening Post, during the following week.

'They want me to go for another interview. Oh dear, I'm not sure what to do,' muttered Lizzie. 'It's what I always wanted, but I'm not sure now.'

Family Ties

Lizzie decided to go for the interview anyway and see what they had to say. It seemed she had been next in line for a job, following her previous interview.

'We'd like to see a sample of your writing, if possible. Have you any experience of writing articles or reports?' the Editor, Mr Apperly asked.

'Well, actually, you recently bought one of my articles for publication. The piece about Cobridge's china?'

'Giles Trentham, I recall. That was you?' Lizzie nodded and grinned. 'Why the name?'

'Cos I didn't think you'd accept it if you knew I was a girl.'

'Are we really so prejudiced?'

'Seems like it to me. You only seem to employ females to be secretaries.'

'You may be right. But if you can write articles like that one, perhaps I was wrong. It's coming out next week, by the way. I was always planning to do a series of articles featuring our wonderful pottery industry. I think we might use this as the start of them.'

'That's excellent. Actually, can I ask you something?'

'Fire away.'

'If I carried on working at Cobridge's, would you take my articles if I sent them in? Only I've got lots of ideas and I do rather enjoy the job I've got.'

He stared at her and then smiled.

'We certainly do take freelance articles from selected contributors. If you like your current job so much, why are you here?'

'Because this was always my dream. But I think I've seen the reality much more clearly. I'm only partly doing secretarial stuff at the factory. I'm much more like an assistant to Mrs Cobridge. And I don't really want to be stuck reporting on scout camps and garden parties. I want to write real stuff. Important things about real people.'

Mr Apperly stared at her and finally laughed.

'One day, Lizzie Vale, I'm sure you'll be a famous writer. Send me your articles. I'm sure we can come to some arrangement. And let's agree right now, that you are really Lizzie Vale and not Giles Trentham.'

'I think I'd like to become known as Elizabeth Vale for my writing.'

'Elizabeth Vale it is. Thanks for coming in. And I'm glad we've sorted things out. I got into trouble with your brother-in-law, James when I didn't give you a job before.'

'You mean this is all because of something he said? You only asked me to come for an interview because of James?'

'Not at all. It was a genuine interview and genuine offer on your own merits. I look forward to meeting you again. More articles on different companies would be most acceptable. You have a knack of putting in just enough details about the people who work there as well as the processes. Do bring in your work the next time. If I'm free, I'll be pleased to discuss it with you.'

They parted amicably and Lizzie left in high spirits. She knew Nellie would be delighted that she was staying with her and wickedly decided to tease her by saying she would be working at the Post from now on.

'Well of course I'm pleased for you, but I shall really miss you,' Nellie said, trying to put a brave face on it. 'And your plans for books and so on, I loved that idea. I've even done a few preliminary sketches. Maybe something can come of them one day, if you've ever got enough time between your reporting.'

'Oh, I'm sorry, Nellie. I shouldn't have teased you. I turned the job down, but he still wants me to write for him, freelance, he called it.'

'You mean you're going to stay here? You wicked girl, leading me on like that. But I'm delighted. We need to celebrate right away. I'm taking you out for a splendid lunch. Get your coat.'

'I've still got it on already, if you only looked. Come on then. No work today. I love it.'

They went to a large hotel on the outskirts of Stoke and ordered a huge meal. Lizzie was glad she'd been to a posh place with Charlie and managed to feel quite at ease, ordering with a confidence which surprised her sister.

'My little sister's really grown up,' she said with a smile.

'I think I have. And I think now I'm ready to announce my own engagement to Charlie. I didn't want to tell anyone 'til I could come to terms with coping with his parents. But now I am sure that he needs me and my lovely family. We will have to manage somehow and there will be lots of things to be sorted out. But there's plenty of time. I'm not even nineteen yet and we have years of peace ahead of us, thank goodness.'

'You're engaged? So when exactly did he ask you to marry him?'

'He asked me a couple of weeks ago and I said yes.'

'And you've kept it to yourself all this time. I'd have been bursting with the news.'

'Oh yes? And who was it got married . . . actually married . . . without telling anybody? You kept that a secret for ages.'

'I suppose we did. But there were reasons for that. Anyhow, congratulations, my dear little sister. I know he'll be the right one for you. Charlie Swift is lovely.'

'I know. I love him, now that I understand what love really means. What a lot has happened this year. It will be nineteen thirty-nine in a few weeks. I wonder what that will bring?'

'Who can tell? At least the threat of another war seems to be over. Mr Chamberlain assured us of that. I hope we shall see Joe and Daisy, happy with their new family. Mum living at Cobridge House. Ben and Jenny with their own little place and you and

Charlie, hopefully with somewhere of your own as well. You know we'll always help you all to find somewhere to live. One good thing about having money, it enables you to help others. And having you working closely with me will make my life much easier.'

'You're a wonder, Nellie. You've always been the heart of this family. Mum always did her best, bless her, but it's you who's really provided for us all from years back. We'd have starved at one time if it hadn't been for you.'

'Thank you, Lizzie. I appreciate your words, but if we don't eat soon, I shall be in tears and the food will go cold.'

'Here's to *family* and the true value of having us all around for each other.' They raised their glasses and drank a toast. 'Just don't let on to Mum that I'm getting a taste for wine. She'd make me sign the pledge right away.'

'Sisters. Here's to sisters. And you're the very best anyone could have.'

Nellie laughed as they both wiped away their tears.

WHERE THE HEART IS
OUT OF THE BLUE
TOMORROW'S DREAMS
DARE TO LOVE

We do hope that you have enjoyed reading this large print book.

Did you know that all of our titles are available for purchase?

We publish a wide range of high quality large print books including:
**Romances, Mysteries, Classics
General Fiction
Non Fiction and Westerns**

Special interest titles available in large print are:
**The Little Oxford Dictionary
Music Book, Song Book
Hymn Book, Service Book**

Also available from us courtesy of Oxford University Press:
**Young Readers' Dictionary
(large print edition)
Young Readers' Thesaurus
(large print edition)**

For further information or a free brochure, please contact us at:
**Ulverscroft Large Print Books Ltd.,
The Green, Bradgate Road, Anstey,
Leicester, LE7 7FU, England.
Tel:** (00 44) **0116 236 4325**
Fax: (00 44) **0116 234 0205**

WOMBAT CREEK

Noelene Jenkinson

Single mother Summer Dalton arrives from New South Wales to her grandfather's small farm in the Western District. However, memories of her hippy parents' banishment for their free-loving morals — decades before — remain. Her hope is to settle on the land she's inherited, so she refuses her new neighbour Ethan Bourke's offer to buy her out. Then, a jealous old flame and Ethan's disapproving mother come into the mix. Can Summer and Ethan resolve their growing attraction to one another?